ROMANCING THE RAINBOW

Enrapturing Tales is an imprint of:

Knight Writing Press
PMB # 162
13009 S. Parker Rd.
Parker CO 80134

KnightWritingPress@gmail.com

DEDICATION

for L.J.

and everyone else who needs it.

Table of Contents

Sugar Spun Hearts

by
Sarah Marie Page

Sugar Spun Hearts

Dear Self (in 5 years),
Her hair is cotton candy and it's the most beautiful thing. She dyed it pink on Thursday. Before that it was a sort of unicorny-purple that brought out the green in her eyes. She wears ripped jeans and t-shirts with dad jokes. A baseball cap backward.

"Where do you think we'll be in five years?" she asks.

With you, I want to say.

We're sitting on the hood of her car outside an ice-cream shop. She's licked hers into a point. Her ice-cream is supposed to be the second tallest building in San Francisco, but a few drops have ruined the illusion.

Strawberry.

It's the color of the books in my bag.

The color of the bruises on her bicep.

The color of sunset or sky or spun sugar.

Her thigh brushes mine, a nudge. My heart skitters.

I jam my hands into the pockets of my sweater. My cup is half-empty. Rainbow sherbet, the colors running together into a muddle of pinkish-brown. *Where do you want to be?* "I don't know." The lie sticks to my teeth, sweet like syrup. "Maybe grad school. You know, Berkeley. Brown."

She lets out a low whistle. "Ivy League. Fancy girl."

"What about you?"

I already know the answer. She wants to be a rockstar, wants to sing up on a stage. Last semester, she dropped out of school to become the vocalist for a band called *The Stinks.* That's why her dad gave her the bruises.

Not for kissing girls.

Never for kissing girls.

She doesn't even like girls. She told me that after we pulled away from each other, swollen lips and hazy eyes.

"I don't like girls," she'd said, breathlessly, tugging at the fringe on her sock.

"I don't like girls." Pressing me backward on the bed.

"I don't like girls." Sneaking me in through the back of the movie theater. That night, she'd said it a thousand times, had squeezed her eyes closed and balled her hands so tight her nails left little half-moon indents on her palm. *I don't like girls, I don't like girls, I don't like girls.*

I wanted to tell her that she's pretty, that her skin smells like grapefruit, that her Pink Floyd tee-shirt is my favorite. I wanted to tell her that her laugh sounds like a wheezing balloon but I love it, I love it so please never stop.

I don't even know if I like girls, but I like her.

A crush is a funny thing. Why do we call it a crush, anyway? It sounds like you're suffocating, like the world is being dropped on top of you and all the air is being pumped out of your lungs. Your eyes bulge and you can't breathe. But when I think of her, I don't think I'm being crushed. I feel soft and warm, like candy or kitten tongues. I feel like floating.

But it's 1989, and we're teetering on the edge, sitting on the cusp. The city lights splinter in front of us, a thousand shimmering parts. A few cars speed past and the neon ice cream sign flicks blue, green, blue, green, blue—

"Hey." She places her hand over mine. Flips it over. Traces the lines of my palm—my life line, my fate line, my heart. I think she's going to tell me she doesn't like girls again.

"You don't have to listen to them," she says instead. Her voice is husky, a little rough.

"To who?"

She shrugs. "Everyone."

"I'm not."

"You are."

"Am *not.*"

She snatches a book from the bag at my hip. "Economics? *Boring.* Do you really want to spend your life studying budgets and"—she flips through the pages—"what the *fuck* are basis points?"

I snatch the book back. "It's interest. On a loan."

"Sounds awful."

"It's economics."

"It's a trap."

"Secret of Nimh?"

"Return of the Jedi." She nudges my shoulder, then makes her voice go nasally. "It's a trap! You hear me? Donna Sheffield it's a trap, it's a trap, it's a trap!"

The car hood warms my legs. The sound of crickets hum through the night.

"No, really," she says. This time her voice is serious. "Where do you want to be?"

Dear Self (in 5 years),

Bachelor's of Applied Economics. BE-con. Berkeley. So many basis points. Graphs and charts. GPA 4.0. Done. *Done.* Then graduate school. Masters of Applied Economics. ME-con. More basis points. Stanford. I haven't slept in two days.

"You need a break," my boyfriend says, wadding up a paper and throwing it at my head.

"I'm a machine." I grab the ball and un-wrinkle it. Douglass North's model for American economics. Good. I need this.

My boyfriend wraps his arms around me and pulls me into bed, smooths my forehead, kisses my hair. We should be right together, cheek on chest, but we fit all wrong, a box of cheap furniture, laminate and plastic glossed to a shine.

"I'm so hard for you right now," he murmurs. His voice has a sleepy lilt. "So hard."

And I can *feel* it, the stiffness of him pressed against my leg.

It's 1994, and I'm sandwiched between two decades, a bug squished between the glass. I can't breathe and maybe this is the way things are supposed to be, but I'm crowning.

I'm drowning.

In papers.

At work.

At school.

But this is what I wanted. This. Right here. Charts and graphs. BEcon. MEcon. Ph.Dcon. This. *This.*

He threads his thumbs through my belt loops, tugs me closer. Now, his hips rest against mine and he's nuzzling my hair. His breath smells like beer and his hands wander down my waist to my butt. My pant buttons.

I squeeze my eyes shut because this is what I wanted. BEcon. MEcon. This is what I wanted. Thi—

Dear Self (in 5 years),
I saw her on TV last night.

Dear Self (in 5 years),
Why is she so beautiful?

Dear Self (in 5 years),
She's touring San Francisco.

Dear xxxxxxxxxx—
The stench of sex and sweat, of summer and dead grass. Stage 4 at 8:30pm. I twist the plastic wristband, the one that says SOUNDSTORM SAN FRANCISCO, and shoulder my way through the crowd. So many people. Baggy jeans and crop tops. Skin that reeks from standing out in the sun, but now it's dark and her show is starting.

Her show. Not *the* show.

The show's been going on since noon, since the security guards threw open the gates to the fairgrounds and started to admit teenagers and twenty-somethings all decked out with piercings and pink hair and, for a second, I wasn't standing on an asphalt parking lot, I was sitting on a car hood. Spun sugar. Pink hair.

Where do you want to be?

The stage lights go black. Titanium. Buzzing.

The strum of a cord, and when the spotlight comes on, she's standing on a raised platform with an electric guitar. The giant screen above us flickers alive.

Red lips, coy smile. "Hello, San Francisco," she says.

The crowd goes wild. It is a wash, a bellow. A sea of cigarette smoke that swallows me whole.

I tug at the cuff of my cardigan. I don't know why I'm here, with a plastic wristband that cost three times as much as my groceries, to listen to someone I kissed once. All I know is that when I sit in my office at UC Stanford, with its oak siding and interior windows, with its packet of documents that says, "Welcome first-year faculty," I feel like I'm sleepwalking.

When I think of her, I'm awake.

We love you, the crowd screams. *We love you, we love you, we love you, we love you, we love you.*

She plays the beginning of one of her songs, then stops. "I'm from SFC. You know that? Born and raised. I usually start with *Neon Dreamscape,* but since I'm from here, I thought I'd start with something else. This song's one of my older ones. It's about rainbow sherbet and strawberry skies. It's about first love and growing up. It's about my…*Maybe Girl.*"

The stage lights turn a buttery yellow. The beginning of *Maybe Girl* is candy-soft, spun sugar and lemon drops. I've heard it—I've heard all of her songs a thousand times, hit *play play play* until the cassette tape burned out.

This time it's different. It's softer, stiller, the metallic edges filed off. She sings it like a secret, says it like a prayer.

She sits on the car hood
Glimpses of her
I can see her silky glances
Can see what we once were
Here's the thing about growing up
They tell you what to be
But I don't ever want to stop
My maybe girl from loving me

When she finishes, she sings another song and another. Five in total and then the lights go black. The platform's gone. The next band prepares to take the stage and the crowd is starting to disperse. I grab a few snapped wristbands and a water bottle someone left behind. There's got to be a trashcan somewhere and suddenly she's here, standing in the middle of the grassy knoll.

"Hey," she says. She's wearing a ripped, black t-shirt that shows off a flat stomach and a hibiscus tattoo. A lanyard marked "*VIP*" hangs around her neck.

"How'd you know I came?"

"Told the security guards to radio if they saw an Econ nerd wandering around. And I...might have also circulated your UC Stanford faculty pic." She smiles and bites her lip. "Do you want to grab a beer? We have some in the back."

I'm floating. I'm floating. I don't want to come back down. I flash my two drink tickets at her. "Might as well use these."

People don't recognize her as we pick our way through the crowd, past the hot dog stand and port-a-potties.

"Do you remember when we were kids, and we'd play the 'where do you want to be?' game?" She glances over her shoulder at the stage. Light gleams off her eyes as the guitarist from *Bleeding Outlaws* rips a wicked solo. "We're there now. We are literally there."

The beer guy hands us two cups.

"Ten years," I say.

"Huh?"

"You always asked where I wanted to be in five. We're in the future now."

She takes a gulp. Bubbles fizz her upper lip like a mustache. "The future? It's a trap!"

"Still quoting *Return of the Jedi*?"

"Every damn day."

"It's a shame you don't like girls." The words come out too fast and I can't believe I'm saying this. I feel silly, stupid, like I'm going to throw up. "We could have been so good together."

Her mouth pulls into that coy smile. "You seriously didn't get any of that?"

"Any of what?"

"The song. The colors. The fact that I sent an army of security guards to look for you. It was literally the most romantic gesture I could think of."

"You didn't want to stop by Stanford?"

"And listen to you talk about basis points?" She shudders for dramatic effect. Then stills. Fiddles with the corner on her plastic VIP badge. "I mean, yeah. I guess I would have. Could you imagine though? I'm pretty sure I'd be thrown out of your hoity-toity building."

I want to tell her it's not hoity-toity. Instead, I say, "I would have let you in."

There's a silence between us, a second. It's 1999, and we're teetering on the edge. She pulls me under the heavy stage lights, just past security and the space partitioned for performers. *Bleeding Outlaws* finishes their set and the world goes wild.

Fireworks burst.

She flips over my palms, traces my lifeline until she finds my heart. There's something mischievous in her eyes. "Alright. Ten years. Where do you want to be? And *please* don't say college professor. I will literally kill you."

I don't want to be a college professor.

I never wanted to be a college professor.

Her hair is cotton candy. It's the most beautiful thing.

I tilt her chin toward mine.

We kiss.

From the Author

When you're graduating high school, you're always asked a thousand times "where do you want to be in 10 years?" As someone who's now living in the future, I think it's so interesting to look back and see what you wanted and compare that to what actually happened.

I also wanted to tip my hat to all the brave individuals who came out before Obergafell and the other legal protections the US government affords to LGBTQIA+ individuals. My husband has two uncles who fell in love in the 1970's, and I look at them and think how incredibly brave they are.

Brett and Don, this one's for you.

About the Author

Sarah Marie Page spends her days engaging in intense battles of wits, fueled by copious amounts of tea and the occasional dramatic slamming of a briefcase. AKA: She's a lawyer.

When she's not doing lawyer things, she can be found sneaking off to make-believe worlds filled with romance, betrayal, and enemies-to-lovers tension. If you liked this piece, she thinks you might like her debut novel, *Illusion of Stars*.

She's also a frequent flier on Instagram.

Check her out: @sarahpagestories.

Lucas & Jack

by
Kevin A Davis

Lucas & Jack

Plodding through the snow, I had only the glimmer of lights ahead to convince me I wouldn't be a man-sized icicle come morning. I might have been able to survive with my werewolf blood, but the first LED twinkling of civilization had put a bit more spring in my step.

The roads were as laden with snow near the town as the highway where I'd left my Nissan Cube. After a long day for the both of us, it had given up in the middle of the storm. I just had to hope something was open in this patch of humanity before I started knocking on doors.

My luck turned as the first building on my right was a volunteer fire station. The man who let me in had a handsome, freshly-shaved face and a brow which wrinkled too easily into a frown. The air was warm, smelled of burgers, and carried the sound of other voices from deeper in the bays.

I forced a smile and wiped snow and frost off my beard. "Thank you." My braid had kept my hair back under the hood.

"Bad night to be out." His tone hinted at my bad planning, or downright stupidity.

"That's for sure." I forced an apologetic smile. "I got stuck out on the highway north of here. I'm Lucas. Is there a hotel in town?"

"Stable Inn's closed, but there's a couple bed and breakfasts down the road. Should be able to map them on your phone."

I was interrupting his cozy night inside, and we both knew it. "Lost my charger. Cell's dead. Can you sketch me directions?" A ride would be out of the question.

He latched the door behind me as I stared from the storm to the hastily scribbled lines. Luckily, the town wasn't very big.

Ten minutes later, I stared at the no vacancy sign on the Pumpkin Patch B&B as the growing storm threatened to bury me if I stood still for any amount of time. Every place in this tiny Vermont village had closed up for the night.

I trudged back out to the street, heading for the only other opportunity with a hope of warmth. According to the sketched map, it was just across the park, but even the leafless trees appeared to be sinking into the rising drifts.

I fought a mounting hope as warm light leaked out of windows tucked under a porch. Red and blue dotted the yellow glow as I strode confidently toward the three-story building. Its high-peaked roof had not been able to shed the new snow. Without tracks in the fresh pile, it took me a moment to find the entrance. From what I could see, the interior appeared more a bar than a hotel. My heart skipped when, through a window, I saw a man talking.

Pale skin highlighted his dark eyes and quick smile. His light blue button-down shirt was open at the collar, and my eyebrows rose when I recognized brightly colored suspenders striped down his chest. Possibly late thirties, he had a fine, trim figure and gestured with both hands as he spoke.

I blinked, stopped ogling, and focused on the door, stomping snow off my boots before I tried the handle. It opened.

Blissfully warm air cocooned me, smelling of beer and popcorn. Light music played in the background, overridden by an energetic voice which I assumed belonged to the man with the suspenders. A bartender moved out of the shadows and wiped the counter as she nodded to me. Most of the multihued lights came from behind the wooden bar; it silhouetted the animated speaker as he stepped from his audience to peer at me.

"Welcome, stranger. Name's Jack, your illustrious host." His tone was light and friendly, though as his expression became visible, he scrutinized me with deep, intense eyes.

I smoothed my face with gloved fingers as I introduced myself. "Lucas. I'm looking for a room for the night. Could you point me to the front desk or—"

Jack cut me off with a wave toward the bartender. "Sorry, no rooms, Tiny. Bar's open for a couple more hours, if we keep power."

At six feet one inches and 180 pounds in my human form, I didn't appreciate the nickname. "Lucas," I corrected.

Jack ignored me, turning back to his audience. He leaned onto the table with one hand, and his lips quirked into a devilish smile as he asked a question of a shaggy, graying man.

My frigid cheeks flushed as I shrugged out of my wet coat. I didn't have a lot of options for the night with my phone dead, but I wasn't about to pass up a chance to get warm, even for a few hours.

Two groups of customers occupied the tables, leaving the inset bar to me alone. I forced the scowl off my face and trod toward a tall chair in front of the bartender. "Do you have a charger?" I pulled my phone out of my jeans and pointed the port toward her.

"Don't, sorry." Brown hair tied in a ponytail she wore a blue and green flannel, thinner than my purple and black mackinaw. "What can I get you?"

Sixteen hours on the road and another one tromping through the snow had me drained. The owner's flippant attitude did nothing to improve my mood. The bar had WhistlePig on the shelf, so I just slid my phone back in my pocket. Getting drunk wouldn't fix my day. "Some type of light beer."

She listed three as she slid a bowl of pretzels across the polished wood toward me.

All light beer tasted like crap, but I needed to nurse something while I thawed out. "Whatever you recommend."

I slumped at the counter as she rattled glasses and poured from a tap. My best plan consisted of asking if I could sleep on the floor of the fire station. Did they even have a police station here? In the morning, after the storm, I could borrow a phone and call for someone to get my car.

I started when a hand slapped down on my shoulder. "What's your story, Tiny?" Jack's annoying grin didn't quite reach his steely eyes. His lips flattened and he patted my shoulder. "Oh."

"Lucas."

Jack pulled a chair up, nodded to the bartender, and smirked. "Tiny Lucas?"

I flattened my right hand onto the bar. "Just Lucas." Belated, his response after his initial statement hit me. "What do you mean, 'oh'?"

He studied my face, a grin reforming. After a quick glance to the mirrors of the bar, he leaned in conspiratorially. "You're a werewolf."

Jack had to be a witch. A regular human wouldn't be able to tell, not when I was in human form. I didn't answer immediately but glanced at the bartender. She had to have heard. "Jackass," I murmured.

"Jack's ass is a very, very fine ass." He actually laughed at his comment, then raised a finger off the bar to point at her. "You don't even want to know."

Did he mean I didn't want to know what she was? Was he trying to irritate me? I needed to thaw out, not get thrown out. "Whatever." As a werewolf, I'd learned early in life not to let my emotions get out of control.

"So, what's your story?" He didn't seem inclined to leave me to my self-pity.

It takes me a minute or two to change gears sometimes, and Jack downright vexed me. However, the bar was warm, and he owned it, or at least ran it. "Car's stuck in the snow about an hour's walk north of here."

The bartender brought a martini for Jack, and my beer. As she dropped the coasters in front of us, the lights went out. A communal groan sounded throughout the room. The bartender swore. My eyes quickly adjusted as she placed our drinks down.

"Generator will kick on," Jack said. He easily found his glass and took a sip, then sighed. "The guests will be complaining. Two lights per room. Catch the phones, will you?"

I thought for a moment he was speaking to me. The bartender answered, "I'll let them know." Her accent was not New England, but I couldn't place it. Maybe California.

"Three." He was smiling at me over the rim of his glass. "Two."

Was he flirting, after being a jerk? I was in no mood.

His last count sounded unsure. "One."

We sat in the dark, his smile slowly fading for a second before he spoke again. "Candles?"

"Got it."

Reluctantly, he placed his glass down and flashed a fake smile. "Want to help?" He slapped my shoulder. "With these drifts, I could use some muscle."

He was hardly unfit himself, but I had a couple inches on him and a few pounds. After technically planning on kicking me out in

18

the weather, I found it annoying that now he wanted my help. I tend to take those kinds of things personally.

I shoved back at my foul mood. It wouldn't kill me to help either. "Sure."

The bartender placed two long flashlights in front of us before returning to her candles. Jack grabbed one, and I slid off the chair and took the other.

"You closing, Jack?" a female voice asked from a murmuring cluster at the closest table. Cell phones were already out, lighting faces in pale blue.

"Not yet. Tiny's going to help me get the generator back on."

The table let out a cheer and glasses clinked. "Tiny!"

I gripped my flashlight as I followed Jack. "Lucas," I corrected, once again.

He stopped at a long black coat hung on a peg. His smirk grew wide, and he lit the flashlight to spotlight his face. "So, not tiny?"

I grabbed my own coat and put up the hood, zipping the front with a sharp yank, and pointedly not answering him. He pulled on what could have been a military coat with epaulettes and quickly buttoned the front. He turned up the collar but didn't wear a hat.

As he opened the door, the chill of the storm hit like ice, even under the porch. The wind wasn't too strong, but the blizzard turned the air white. Drifts piled higher than my knees. I couldn't see anything beyond two, maybe three yards. Even in this form, my sight would be better than most humans'. Maybe everybody would be stuck at the bar and Jack would leave the room open.

Jack led; even if I could see better, as he would know his own property. I hoped. Then again, he wasn't even wearing a hat. At least he'd been bright enough to put on gloves.

A gust whistled into us as we turned a corner. I had no sense of direction yet, but I felt like we were heading behind the three-story building. Cars were parked to our left, their shapes softened under piles of snow.

"I'm guessing you can see better than me," Jack yelled. "The generator is in a small shed at the end of these buildings."

I could make out a fence maybe, no buildings. "You know where you're going though?"

"One could hope." Jack kept humor in his tone. "But the generator is supposed to kick on automatically and look how well that went."

He might be an idiot, or at least not take anything seriously. Snow flurried into my hood, cold and wet against my neck. I tugged it tighter with gloved fingers. How Jack managed an inn and tavern escaped me. Did his customers actually find him humorous?

The wind carried a sharp cracking snap, muffled in the storm. "Did you hear that?"

"Hear what? I don't have your ears, Tiny." We passed the last car-shaped mound and Jack paused, then veered left. "Can you see anything ahead, maybe to the left?" His steps were hesitant.

I rankled slightly at his return to his nickname for me. I could bear his stupidity, if there was a chance of shelter for the night. A dark, round shape formed to our right, and the crack sounded again. "Over there. A bush maybe." He followed as I moved toward it.

"Shouldn't be a bush in the parking lot." His flashlight swept from side to side.

It was definitely a plant with dark green tones which rose above my head. "Don't you even know your own property?"

"The cozier parts, for sure."

"It's a pine tree." The angle was wrong, and the snow had been shaken off the needles. "The top of one. Could it have fallen and taken down your lines?"

"Likely." He smacked a branch dusting off flakes of snow. "There are a few trees back here."

"Let's find your generator." I turned us back in the direction we'd been going.

It only took a few steps to confirm my worry. I pointed down the dark trunk angling up into the white flurries. The tilt told me the base leaned on something. "Can you see that?" I asked.

"The tree which might be crushing my shed? Yeah, pretty much."

So, Jack wasn't an idiot. He'd also managed one response without a snarky comment or ill-timed humor. I glanced at him as we followed the fallen tree back to the source. His hair stuck to his head and snow melted into it. "Why would you not wear a hat?"

His smile grew when he found me studying him. "Static. Totally ruins my look. I do better with wet and wild."

I grunted and focused my flashlight on the tree trunk. Its angle had lifted the bottom about knee height, so it cleared the snow.

"Nice of you to care, Tiny." Jack's tone was far too perky for the situation.

"I don't." I considered the fire station again. At least the man there wouldn't be obnoxious. He likely wouldn't talk to me at all.

The shed, or what was left of it, came into my view. The tree had flattened the middle of it to half its height. I said nothing as we approached. The trunk ended in splinters just past the remains of the building.

Jack leaned down and slid under the trunk. "Door's on the far side."

"What's the point?" The storm had destroyed his generator, he'd have to wait until power was restored.

"No harm in trying. There are going to be some nervous, maybe even scared people." Jack's tone sounded serious for once, as if he cared.

There wouldn't be much benefit in opening the door, let alone getting inside, since the metal puckered in toward the middle. Still, I scraped under the trunk, unavoidably snagging my hood and shifting it off. As I stood and fixed my coat, Jack jingled keys as he cornered the building. The side tilted in toward the center. I found him leaning in with one hand bracing against the slanting wall and unlocking a padlock attached to a buckled door.

"It opens outward," he said.

I shook my head. "It used to."

The lock clicked open, and Jack peered up with a grin. "Was that humor, Tiny? You amaze me at every turn." He retrieved his lit flashlight from his coat pocket.

I ignored his jibe and waited as he tried the knob and yanked. The door barely rattled. My petty side enjoyed his frown.

His head swiveled to gaze at me, and a light grin crept on his lips. "You're enjoying this, aren't you?"

I forced myself not to smile. "A little."

"C'mon, Muscles." He stepped back, gesturing to the door. "Give it a try."

"Lucas." I didn't move, except to shine my flashlight into his face.

He winced and blocked the light with his hand. "Can you even drink milk?" he asked.

"What?"

"Before you sour it?" He made sure to adjust his hand so I could see his smile. "Alright, *Lucas*, would you be so kind as to use some of those hunky muscles to pry open this door? I doubt I can do anything with the generator, but I should at least try."

He was right. If we came all the way out here, we should at least see, and he had called me by my name. As he held both flashlights, I used one hand inside the mangled opening and the other on the knob. The door screeched open.

The generator would not be running any time soon. The roof and trunk leaned their full weight into it, indenting the outer casing and causing the wiring panel to bulge out. The gas lines leading into the ground were undamaged or I would have smelled the gas long ago.

"Gas heating?" I asked with some level of self-interest.

Jack nodded, still prodding at the broken generator. "Thankfully. Beds will be warm, but there'll be no water or lights for a while. I'll have to kick everyone out in the morning." His once tousled hair clung to his head, likely attempting to freeze.

"Does that include me?" Surely, he'd let me rest out the storm, now that I'd helped him.

A smirk turned to a leer as he trailed the flashlight up my body. "No." The beam of light stopped on my chest, just short of shining in my eyes. "You can stay longer."

I flushed slightly and turned toward the slanted doorway. "Thanks. Morning will be fine." The storm had already dusted into the shed as if searching for us.

Jack likely flirted with everyone he met. It seemed his nature. I couldn't take him seriously. Shelter until morning I would gratefully accept. His offer peeled off some of my moodiness.

"Well, I can't do any damage here. We might as well get back." He stood and wiped off his head with a gloved hand. If I'd had a hat, I would have given it to him.

I tightened my hood and stepped outside. The blizzard seemed heavier and colder. Each step in the drifts brought my knee up to my hips.

Jack led us back along the tree trunk, the opposite side from which we came instead of trying to squeeze under it. We navigated around a stray branch, half-hidden in the snow. When we got to the top of the tree, Jack angled to the right and stomped off. The snow fell so densely, I barely could make out his dark coat.

I searched for any sign of our previous footsteps. The blizzard couldn't have filled them in already. "I don't see our tracks."

"We're fine. It's a parking lot. We can't actually get lost."

After a dozen more steps, I double-stepped to come up to his side. "Are you sure you know where we're going?"

He pointed forward with a shiver. "That way."

I frowned. Humans didn't do well in freezing weather. "You're cold."

"Okay. A hat might have been a prudent idea. I'm not good with those."

"Hats?"

"Prudent ideas."

I smiled, grateful that he wouldn't see it. Lights were our best hope. We _were_ in a town, so technically we'd find a building eventually.

Ahead and to the left, a shadow hinted at some form. I pointed. "There's something over there."

Jack nodded. His shoulders curled up at his neck and his face had turned a harsh pink. I needed to get him out of the cold before he ended up with frostbite.

We were walking toward a tree, and more were taking shape behind it. Had we reached the park? "It's trees."

"Goddess, I must have circled to the back. There's nothing but forest back here." Jack stamped his feet and turned back the way we came. Our footprints barely showed.

"Big parking lot?" I asked.

He shivered and nodded. "The trees start on the south side. If we continue along them, we should get to the Andersons' house. I can bring us along the interior of the parking lot from there." Jack gestured randomly. "Then back over to the inn. We'll make it."

"You're sure?"

"Pretty much. Unless we're over on the west end…"

Alone, I would survive, if uncomfortably. But Jack could end up hurt before we finally returned. The other option I didn't like. "I could partially transform. My sight and smell are much better. Which direction do you expect the inn to be at?"

Jack pointed directly back along our tracks. "In that direction. I'm guessing."

He didn't argue with my offer. It would decrease the time he'd have to spend in this weather. Grunting, I knelt to unlace my boot.

He stomped in place while he waited. "So, how much do you need to strip off?"

Handing him a boot, I plunged my dry, woolen sock into the snow and felt the cold seep in immediately. I moved quicker unlacing the second. "Not much."

"Pity."

My second boot I handed to him once I stood. The cold moist of snow had begun wetting the first sock. I unzipped my coat and handed it to him. "You might as well wear this, at least it has a hood."

He mocked an offended expression. "With this coat and boots?"

I unbuttoned my thick mackinaw, pointedly ignoring his prying eyes. Other than a few unfortunate times, I avoided transmogrifying in front of others, especially humans, witch or not. Semi-transformed, I could wear human clothes, but the upper chest would be tight while the hips were small.

Grabbing my belt, I reached for the wolf. Transmogrification can happen very quickly, but it is best to move slowly when aiming for a semi transformed state. It just stretches out the pain.

The most agonizing part, to me, started at the jaw and rippled across the side of my skull. My ribs reshaping caused a numbness along the torso and hips because of their impact on the spine and the alteration of nerve clusters. As legs and arms lengthened, pain sparked at the joints. My pants loosened, staying on only because I held them in growing claws. Muscles and ribs opened my shirt, exposing thickening fur to the snow. My socks tightened with my nails but loosened around the ankles. I might lose them.

The world shifted into a tighter focus, and I could smell elements of Jack clearly from the musk of his groin to the false perfume of his shampoo. With long, thick nails, I tried to readjust my buckle.

"Here, let me help." Jack reached for my belt. He'd tied my boot laces together and draped them over his shoulders. So much for style.

His nimbler, human fingers managed the buckle much easier than my long nails. I sniffed the breeze as he worked. From my right, I caught the scent of fire. Just below that, Jack with his musk, alcohol, and soap rising sharpest. I pushed that to the back of my mind. In this form, my emotions were always more difficult to restrain.

He finished and gazed up at me, resting one hand on my chest. "I'm more adept at taking belts off than putting them on."

I snorted, then pointed in the direction of the oncoming wind. "Fire." My voice sounded like stepping in fine gravel.

"Okay. It might be one of the fireplaces." He shrugged and gestured with the flashlight for me to lead. "At the worst, we'll cause a nice fright to one of my neighbors." My coat remained draped over his arm.

Scents of petroleum mixed with the smoke, but separate, as if cars parked by a building. I still couldn't see far enough through the blizzard.

"Ease up, Tiny."

I turned, pausing, and Jack stomped through the drifts to catch up. If we were out here much longer with the snow building, he wouldn't be able to walk very well at all.

The wind shifted for one brief moment, and I caught two odors which made me smile, urine and alcohol.

Jack's eyes widened. "Is that a smile? I hope it is. Goddess, that's scary." His tone carried his playful tone, but it still made me turn from him.

I shouldn't care what he thought of me.

"Better scent?" he asked, huffing slightly.

Stepping slowly, I focused into the white maelstrom ahead. The wind had shifted, but I knew where the other smells had come from. In three steps, the scent of urine wafted past again, confirming my target.

Jack stayed behind me, likely using the path I left. "So, what do you like to read?"

Did he always need to be talking? I was reading *Godfire* at the moment, but I couldn't imagine how the title would sound with my present capacity for speech. We could chat, later.

"Leigh Bardugo, myself. Read much, Tiny?"

I growled.

"Figured you did. Brooding type who likes to keep your feelings repressed. Takes things personally."

Glaring at him, I stopped.

Jack offered an impish grin, but I saw him shiver. "Don't let me distract you." His hair was stiff and his cheeks too red.

I needed to get him back inside. Jack might be annoying, but I wouldn't be okay with him freezing to death outside. In this form or as a wolf, I could survive. It didn't feel that cold. But he could slip into hypothermia or even just lose parts to frostbite. To help him, I could ignore his jibes.

It took six more steps before I could make out the flickering lights. Jack didn't notice, as he'd gone on to a monologue on his current opinion of the proper usage of mint in alcoholic beverages. The snow drifts had grown to cover his knees, making it near impossible for him to use anything other than my footprints when the shape of the house loomed ahead of us.

I glanced at Jack to see if he'd noticed yet, but he just thought I was interested in his last comment. "I know. You're thinking I've put too much thought into ice cream, especially on a night like tonight, but you can't mix butterscotch with mint chocolate. There's something unnatural about that. Present company excluded."

It took until I had turned us toward the steps of porch when he finally spotted the lights. "Tiny, you did it!"

Whoever had come out for a piss wasn't in sight. Their scent hung heavy to my left. I plodded up the steps quietly and moved away from the window before I fumbled at the belt.

Jack placed my boots and coat on the low drifts of the porch. He knelt and loosened the buckle while shivering. "Now we're talking."

I knew he was just flirting, despite being near frostbite. As I snapped back to my human form in mere seconds, the pain shot me rigid, filling out my pants and leaving the heavy mackinaw flapping in the breeze. "Go inside." My throat grated but sounded more human like. "I'll be right behind you."

Jack nodded and headed for the door. I dressed as a cheer went up from within the inn. His voice rang out above the others, but beyond the tone of his humor, I couldn't make out the words.

When I entered with soggy socks in my boots, Jack stood among a crowd of seven regaling them with a tale of the harrowing trip to the ruined generator. He gazed over with a smile but kept talking. Few of his audience gave me a glance.

"…crushed to the core. The good news is, we've got plenty of candles and heat to last the night. Bad news, ladies, no toilets until the well pump has electricity." Jack hadn't shed his coat and he kept rubbing his face.

I hung up my coat. My mackinaw was wet.

"I can pee in the bushes," one of the women said.

Jack laughed. "I don't doubt it. I'm going to enjoy the heat a bit before I even think of going back out there."

"Here, let me warm you up." She rubbed his cheeks and stood on her tiptoes to kiss him.

Jack didn't stop her. I turned toward the bartender. She watched me with a candle flickering shadows across her face. Perhaps Jack was pansexual. It didn't matter. I hadn't come here for romance. Jack had his friends. Our drinks were gone from the bar, but I headed there anyway.

The bartender reached for a beer glass, and I shook my head. "WhistlePig."

She almost smiled. The gaggle behind me continued with Jack's cheerful voice rising to the top. The bartender gave me the glass, returned the pretzels, and added a candle in a short red container. "Thanks," she said.

I tried to ignore the chattering, swigged the whiskey, and handed the glass back to her. "Still no electricity."

She had the bottle close. "I meant, bringing him back alive. He can be a fool."

Raising the glass, I nodded. At least I'd have someplace warm for the night. Jack focused on his friends. I'm not sure what more I had expected. In the morning, I could find a local tow company for my car, maybe get a nearby hotel, in a real town. I paused, drink at my lips. "He needs a hat."

The bartender glanced behind me and smirked. "And some brains to put in it."

The little group laughed at some quip of Jack's, and I drank half my glass. I hadn't come here to hook up. His bar, his rules. He was a flirt, and nothing more. Tomorrow, Jack and this town would be in my rearview mirror. I finished my drink and tapped the glass on the counter.

Beside me, Jack scraped his chair across the floor to climb in it. "Where were we? Yes, your story."

I jerked a thumb to his customers; they'd settled at their candlelit tables. "Isn't that more interesting?"

"Hardly. I've known them for months, some years. You are far more intriguing, Tiny. This whole repressed emotion thing totally has me hooked." Despite his frivolous tone, his eyes searched mine. "I need to know more. You're like an opening mystery in a Maberry novel. I just need to dig deeper until it's solved. Tell me about your day. How did you end up driving through here? Walking, I mean. C'mon, Tiny." He poked me in the arm as the bartender dropped a coaster and placed a fresh martini on it.

Jack didn't reach for it, his eyes locked on mine. Beyond all his gregarious behavior, joking flirtation, and annoying humor, there was something genuine and caring about him.

"Well, my day hasn't turned out as bad as it started." I put my whiskey down.

I took the annoying jerk's head in both of my hands, and he grinned before I kissed him. I finally shut him up as he leaned into our embrace.

From the Author

Lucas and Jack have been a couple who've been chattering about in my brain for a while now. When I heard of the opportunity to help the wife of L.J., who has added so much to the community, I wanted this anthology to be where they first met. While waiting for *Romancing the Rainbow* to begin its path to being published, Lucas and Jack joined another anthology on a buddy trip a short while after this story.

I can't think of a better place for them to meet than in an anthology which can help others.

About the Author

Kevin A Davis is a contemporary fantasy author with three published series including the Khimmer Chronicles, the AngelSong series, and the paranormal procedural DRC Files, where the adept Kristen is quick to use her magic and wits. Residing in north Florida, he attends conventions throughout the southeastern US either as a vendor, speaker, staff, or a nerdy fan.

He publishes anthologies through Inkd Pub. (www.inkdpub.com) At the annual JordanCon in Atlanta, he is Director of the Authors Workshop track which focuses on hands-on panels for new writers.

You can find his schedule, releases, or join his newsletter at www.kevinarthurdavis.com.

Facebook:
https://www.facebook.com/KevinArthurDavis/
Instagram:
https://www.instagram.com/kevinarthurdavisauthor/

Dark Hearts

by
Sam Knight

Dark Hearts

Humor doesn't work when things aren't funny." Marge's Eastern European accent was heavy, her words clipped, making her sound angry to Stacy, as usual.

"It does. That's what dark humor is," Stacy countered.

"No." Marge shook her head. "That's what insensitivity is."

"No." Stacy shook her head, scowled exaggeratedly, and spoke the word in exactly the same way Marge had, a near perfect imitation refined by a month of practice. She smiled at Marge, trying to let her know she had been teasing. Her voice softened into her own Southern United States accent. "Insensitivity is numbness. Apathy. A lack of caring at all. Dark humor is a way of coping with the fact that you *do* care, that you care *too much* to be dealing with the bad shit that is going on around you."

Marge rearranged the last two cards in her hand, taking a moment to fidget with them, looked at the ones already played on the table between them, and then scratched her head. Her short black hair was just long enough to flow in the zero-g as though she were sitting under water. She played one of the cards, pressing to stick it to the table, and let go of the last one, leaving it to float in the air in front of her, and continued the conversation. "So, the police in your country say those horrible things not because they're prejudiced or racist, but because they feel bad for the people they arrest and beat up? But they beat them up anyway."

"No. The humor is to cope with the situation the police are in. They feel like they are in a lose-lose situation. They are trying to help people who don't want to be helped, or feel like the cops are the enemy, so they resist being helped by them."

"Riiiiiight."

Stacy shrugged. "I mean, not all cops are nice people—were nice people. But my point was dark humor, not the dark side of humanity. Think doctors and nurses instead of cops. They use dark humor to cope, too." She laid a card on top of the last one Marge had played. "I realize it was mostly soldiers where you were, but I'm sure they had dark humor, too."

"They had a sickness. Sickness of mind and soul. They did terrible things to people, and they liked it. There was no humor there. Only horror. Only depravity. Demons on Earth."

Stacy didn't have an answer for that.

After a moment, Marge quickly played her last card. "Okay. Say something funny and dark."

"If I'm going to die all alone out here, I'm glad it's with you." Stacy laid down her last card, let Marge see it for a moment, and then picked up the pile using her fingernails to release the ones adhered to the table.

Marge stared for a moment at where the cards had been. "Damn."

"Funny, right? But dark."

"No. That wasn't funny. I'm just disappointed that you're now an even hundred games ahead on a game *I* taught *you*." Marge tapped the screen built into the table and recorded the win.

"You'll catch up." Stacy started shuffling the cards, expertly controlling them despite the lack of gravity. She paused to catch a long, stray brown hair, one of her own, out of the air.

"Not if I kill you first." Marge's voice was icy.

Stacy froze and looked into Marge's eyes. They were dark and cold, like the empty night of space in the window beyond. "Now that," Stacy said, "was funny." She stuck the hair to the table so it wouldn't end up in her nose. She'd clean it up later.

Marge shook her head. "Is it still funny if it's not a joke?"

"It is if someone thinks it is."

"I don't get that."

"Think of a monkey throwing poo at the zoo. The person getting hit doesn't think it's funny, but everyone else does."

"I don't."

"It was an example."

"Give me a better one."

"It's like schadenfreude—"

A quiet, electronic beep broke the endless silence as surely as if it had been a gong.

"Wanna go watch?" Stacy asked.

"You know I live for it," Marge said.

Stacy packed the cards away. "Was that supposed to be funny?"

"I don't know."

"It kind of was. It was pretty sarcastic, too. I liked it."

"I'm trying." Marge released her seatbelt and pushed off, floating through the common area of the shuttle, heading toward the cockpit. "Socializing isn't really my thing."

"I noticed." Stacy, right behind her, waited for Marge to settle into the captain's seat before rotating herself and pushing her body into the navigator's spot. They sat in silence, looking out of the viewport as the gray, pockmarked lunar surface slowly rotated past below them.

Stacy tilted her head to look at Marge. The glowing crescent rising on the horizon reflected coldly in the woman's dark eyes as she stared into infinity, and Stacy, not for the first time, wondered how dark Marge's heart truly was.

An icon began flashing on the HUD, indicating their shuttle was attempting to make contact with the ascending planet.

"Do you really want to kill me?" Stacy asked. "Is that why it's not funny?"

Marge continued to sit still, unblinking, watching as the top of the bright orb emerged over the horizon. When the Earth finally came fully into view, and they could see the dark smudges of ash smeared across the face of the continents, she spoke. "I don't know. No. But I've thought about it." She finally turned to look at Stacy. "Haven't you?"

"Thought about you killing me? Yeah. I thought you were going to do it a long time ago. In fact, I thought you were going to kill me the day we met, before all this happened. You looked so mean with that perpetual dark scowl of yours. I mean, resting bitch face doesn't even come close to describing it."

Marge scowled.

Stacy, not knowing if the look was intentional or not, chuckled. "But I haven't thought about killing you, no. I don't want to be alone. Thought about killing myself a time or two, maybe, but… That's why they picked us for this, right? Because we have the opposite of suicidal tendencies. We're born survivors. Strong loners who do well alone. And since we aren't interested in sex or romance, we won't cause messy interpersonal problems."

"There is a strong irony there," Marge said, not taking her eyes off the planet drifting so impossibly far away from them. "We are maybe the last two human beings alive, and neither one of us has any base desire to procreate, even if we could."

Stacy gave a small shrug. "I can't imagine changing diapers in zero-g anyway. Little drops of formula and piss floating everywhere."

"Formula, huh? Is that what's wrong with you? No mama's milk?"

"I'm lactose intolerant, so I figure my kid would be, too."

Marge finally took her eyes off the lusterless celestial body and looked at Stacy. "So, you've thought about having kids?"

"Thought about it. Thought about adopting more. You?"

"Adopting, mostly. Not the sex thing…" Her scowl deepened and she looked away again.

"Was that you imagining having sex with me?" Stacy laughed out loud this time. "Damn, woman. Way to make me feel special."

"It's not just you. The idea of sex just disgusts me. Germs, bodily fluids, the smell…"

"Ug. You're gonna gag me now. It doesn't gross me out—well, it didn't use to!—I just don't have any interest."

They sat in silence for a while. The Earth crept higher, until it began to disappear from sight at the edge of the viewport. The icon on the HUD continued to flicker: a fervent, anxious, irrelevant triviality in an unhurried, uncaring universe slowly spinning outside the window.

"Another irony," Marge said as the planet vanished. "I thought I was coming up here, close to Heaven, to find my own little haven where I really almost never had to deal with people. Now…" Her gaze followed the blank space on the wall where the Earth would have been had she still been able to see it. "Now, there are no other people, and I am stuck in here with you, cursed to never be alone until my end."

Stacy looked away. The cockpit was much darker without the pallid light from the Earth shining in.

"Are you avoiding me?" Marge called into Stacy's bunk. "Or did you decide to kill yourself?" After three days, the sound of her own voice was loud, alien.

When no answer came, Marge continued talking. "I know you are not dead. I can't smell you. And it is too hot when we are in the sun for you not to smell."

She waited, but still no reply.

"I apologize in advance, but I am going to invade your personal space just in case you are in need of assistance and cannot ask for it."

"I'm fine!" Stacy finally called out. "Go away."

"If that is what you want." Marge pushed off the wall and floated back toward her own bunk.

Stacy hesitated mid sip as Marge floated into the mess hall.

"Oh. I am sorry," Marge said. "I did not mean to interrupt." She caught hold of the wall and spun herself around to head back.

"Wait," Stacy said.

Marge stopped and looked back at her.

"You are welcome to stay. If you want."

"Are you sure? You seemed to want to be alone."

Stacy lowered the squeeze pouch of mushed carrots. "I was trying to give you space. I know you wanted to be alone."

"Ah. I see." Marge slowly rotated to face her. "You were making yourself a martyr. Suffering all alone so that you could make me happy and make yourself happy at the same time by being superior."

"No!" Stacy made a face as she objected.

"As long as we are being honest," Marge said, "I have something I want to say. You know, before you decide you want to be alone again. I may have resting bitch face, but you have back-stabbing smile."

Stacy gaped, but Marge continued before she could say anything.

"That is why I did not like you when we met. You smile at everyone. It means nothing. It means you cannot be trusted."

"I—" Stacy couldn't find the words to respond. When she didn't say anything more, Marge spoke again.

"It was a poor judgment based upon superficial appearances and cultural differences. You seem a good person. People in my country who smile too much at strangers are predatory."

Nodding, Stacy said, "I'm sorry. I did the same. Judging you, I mean. I assumed that you were being actively hostile when you were merely being reserved."

They looked at each other for a moment, long enough to become uncomfortable.

"Join me?" Stacy asked, gesturing to the open seat across the table.

Marge nodded and pushed off the wall. "What's for breakfast? More banana toothpaste?"

"My real name is Margareta, but I got tired of people calling me Margarita."

"Mine is just Stacy. I always wished it had been short for Anastasia or something exotic, but my parents were…unsophisticated."

Marge played her last card and a flicker of a smile flashed across her lips.

"Was that it?" Stacy asked. "Did you finally catch me?"

Marge tapped the table and recorded the score. "No. I am one ahead."

Laughing, Stacy unbuckled and pushed out of the seat, stretching her body as she floated up. "That's just like you to let a milestone sneak up and blow right on past without letting me know until we hit the next one."

Collecting the cards, Marge flashed a real smile at Stacy.

An electronic beep sounded.

Marge glanced at Stacy, whose face remained impassive. Putting the cards away, Marge said, "I think it's time we do something with the rest of the crew."

"Like what?"

"A funeral. A service of some kind. A burial at space, like a burial at sea."

"Why?" Stacy asked. "What good would that do?"

"For starters, it would let me stop thinking about them every time that chime sounds. Stop imagining their bodies floating in the hold."

"Yeah." Stacy nodded. "And, while we're at it, maybe we should see if we can disable the chime?"

"That would be nice."

The top of the Earth appeared on the horizon. Though clouds dotted it, almost no land or smoke marred this side of the brilliant blue sapphire.

They watched in eerie silence as the whole sphere slowly rose into view.

"'Big blue marble' doesn't do it justice," Marge said. "But I don't have anything better."

"After all these months, I would have thought that I would have become inured to the sight of it," Stacy agreed, "but it still takes my breath away."

"Marge?"

"Mmm?"

"Can I hold your hand?" Afraid Marge would say no, Stacy kept her grip on the seat's arms.

Marge's expression didn't change, but she turned her hand palm-up and held it out. Stacy took it, holding it gently, afraid Marge would pull back if she did anything wrong, and looked back out into the eternal night.

After a long silence, Marge asked, "Are we dating now?"

Stacy's heart fluttered at the thought, and she laughed nervously. Marge's hand in hers felt hot, strange, and perfect, like she never wanted to let go.

Marge looked at her, an uncharacteristic twinkle in her eyes. "Good. I feel the same way."

"What?" Stacy, even more nervous now, laughed again, but realized she was more afraid Marge might pull her hand away.

"Excited. Nervous. Scared," Marge said. "Those are all the things a first date is supposed to feel like, right?"

"I guess? I never really dated before. I mean, I did a couple of times, kind of. I even had sex once, but…" Stacy searched for the words.

"But it didn't matter?" Marge offered. "It wasn't important? It didn't mean anything?"

"Yeah. I guess. More than that. Or less. I was just doing it because it was expected of me. I didn't really want to."

"I understand that. I never wanted to date before either."

Stacy felt herself flush. "And you want to now?"

Marge looked into Stacy's eyes and squeezed her hand. "This is different. I feel very close to you. You have come to mean a lot to me. I…I appreciate you."

Stacy squeezed Marge's hand back. "I feel the same way. Thank you."

They both turned back to look at the Earth, filling the middle of the viewport now.

"Do you suppose there is anyone left?" Stacy asked.

"No one who can answer."

The silence of space filled the cabin.

As the Earth reached the edge of the window, Stacy whispered, "Are you sure you want to do this?"

"Do we have any choice? There is no food left. We have tried everything we can think of. Even if we could go someplace, there doesn't seem to be anyplace to go to. And I think we should stop while I am ahead."

"Is that dark humor?" Stacy chuckled.

"I've been practicing in my room."

"Well, to be honest, I don't really ever want to play cards again."

"Wish granted!"

Laughing, Stacy looked back to the Earth and watched as it slipped out of view. The cabin fell into a dusky light, broken only by the flashing icon that never received an answer.

After forever, Stacy felt her hand grow sweaty in Marge's, and she became self-conscious of it, reluctantly pulling it away and wiping it on her pants. "Sorry," she whispered.

Marge looked at her with soft eyes. "You don't have to apologize to me. You have been more to me than anyone else ever has."

Stacy fought back tears. "I have been told that I can't feel real love, but that's not true. I know that because I love you, Margareta. Once upon a time, I told you that if I'm going to die all alone out here, I'm glad it's with you. I know it sounds terrible, but...I guess that's true."

Letting out a giant sigh, Marge said, "I go searching all the way to the end of the world to find a place where people won't bother me, and instead I find love."

Shaking her head, Marge pulled out a tiny box from her pocket and opened it. Two pills were held in place in foam. She took one out and held it out to Stacy. "This one is mine," Marge said. "I would like to ask you to do me the honor of giving it to me."

A small sob escaped Stacy's throat, and tears formed on her eyelashes. "I would be honored." Her voice was raspy as she reached out to take the pill. "And I would ask that you do the same for me."

Marge nodded and removed the other pill. She held her hand out to Stacy's mouth, and Stacy did the same, reaching to Marge's. They both opened their mouths and took the pills while looking into each other's eyes.

Marge held out her hand. Stacy took it.

They leaned back in the seats.

"You're shaking," Stacy whispered, and squeezed Marge's hand tightly.

"I'm a little nervous. I've never gone all the way on a first date before."

Stacy laughed. "Now *that's* dark."

From the Author

"Dark Hearts," like many things I write, started from a simple idea and then went places I didn't expect it to go. Originally, I was exploring the idea of the (possibly) last two humans alive being trapped on the International Space Station together, each feeling that the other's people were responsible for the destruction of the Earth and hating each other for it.

I think you can still see traces of those origins in the story. But, as I wrote it, the real story, for me, came out. That happened when I started thinking about dark humor. Used by humans, for likely all of human history, to cope with terrible things, dark humor always walks the tightrope of being horribly offensive. And yet, it also helps to create some of the closest bonds between people.

My experiences as an author have allowed me to be fortunate enough to meet many different people, and that has expanded my horizons as a human being, and yet, there are many things I don't understand, things I probably can't understand. But that doesn't mean I can't accept (most of) them, or that I can't try to understand.

I have friends and acquaintances who identify as Ace and Aro which, to me, seemed to clearly mean "not interested." And yet, some of them are in strongly committed, deeply emotional, permanent relationships, which I thought felt counterintuitive.

So, of course, I asked about it. I'm a writer. That's what we do. That was when I learned the term 'queerplatonic.' And that's when I had another, "Oh. I'm an idiot," moment.

People are people are people. All relationships are really pretty much that simple when you break them down into what people need and want from each other and the world around them.

As I wrote "Dark Hearts," and explored the idea of dark humor as a shared bonding experience, I realized that I was looking at one of the many ways these relationships have always formed. How best friends are made. How life-partners are made.

I have to be honest, it was when I heard a voice in my head saying, *"Hello, I'm Jay, and this is my hetero life mate, Silent Bob,"* that it really made perfect sense to me. Thanks, Kevin Smith.

About the Author

Sam Knight is the owner/publisher of Knight Writing Press and author of six children's books, five short story collections, four novels, and over 75 stories, including three co-authored with Kevin J. Anderson.

Though he has written in many cool worlds, such as Jack L. Chalker's Well World, Planet of the Apes, Wayward Pines, and Jeff Sturgeon's Last Cities of Earth, among his family and friends he is, and probably always will be, best known for writing *Chunky Monkey Pupu*.

Once upon a time, Sam was known to quote books the way some people quote movies, but now he claims having a family has made him forgetful—as a survival adaptation.

He is currently working on getting his next novel of The Abandoned Lands published. *A Girl and Her Velociraptor* takes place in a world where dinosaurs have overrun large parts of the Western United States. And where a girl, Xan, and her Velociraptor, Booger, are doing their best to protect their ranch from the bad guys.

To learn more, you can find him at samknight.com.

Threading Die

by
Chris Paranicas

Threading Die

W hen psychotherapists like myself aren't busy modeling clear boundaries, they can occasionally be found in Baltimore bars stalking their plumbers. Everyman's Taproom, known to some locals as "the Every," is an unassuming establishment located in the Mount Vernon neighborhood of the city. It can be described as a chill, mixed bar that turns completely gay after 10pm on Saturdays.

My parents had abandoned, I mean asked me to take care of, a 1940's Cape Cod flanked by Norway maples. They had decamped to Fort Lauderdale to live larger. The first time Travis came to the house to fix something, he seemed a bit out of his depth. One of the outside spigots was leaking and even I knew the solution would involve soldering. He assessed it warily, called home base, and over a protracted interval managed to install a section of pristine copper pipe that made a right turn and exited through the wall. In the process, he partially liquefied a plastic cabinet organizer that I later found in a bathroom sink clamped with metal tongs.

He was employed by a mid-sized company, but I requested him every time. I imagined the crew he ate lunch with razzed him about the kind of customer who expressed an employee preference when they phoned in a problem. Over two years, he restored some functionality, made mistakes, and forgot tools he would circle back to collect.

One day, when Travis was wrapping up, drying the floor with paper towels using his work boot, he turned, and we briefly made eye contact. I was standing at attention several feet away, with some dollar bills in my hand. He waved them off as he passed and said he would be at the Every around 9 on Saturday. I was about to say, "have fun," when I realized that, like in a science fiction movie, a wormhole had just opened up that would transport me to the other side of the universe if I dared to climb in.

In reality, I was about to apply for a completely different role in his life. Rifling through my closet, I pulled out everything that said "athletic." But then sentences from therapy sessions like, "be yourself on dates or otherwise you'll have to act instead of live," pushed into my thoughts. I ended up taking my own advice and wore khaki pants and a blue silk shirt. Showing up in cleats would have been more comical than anything else.

My good feeling about him dated back to our first spigot together, but I never really expected there would be a way to breach the barrier.

A woman near the bar smiled at me while my eyes adjusted. I interpreted it a bit wishfully as a thumbs up. Travis was watching hockey, in blue jeans and a flannel shirt, with his back to me. He had a stocky build that would make him a popular teammate in a tug-of-war, and his blond hair was cut short. I crossed the room and tapped him on the shoulder.

"Hey Wiley." He said it like we met regularly to knock back a few and had been wondering what was keeping me. I had learned during our acquaintance that Travis was forty-one, two years older than me, but it seemed the other way around by more than that. Then again, he had some gray in his hair that I couldn't argue with.

My hunches only got me so far and I opened with, "Do you ever stay past 10?"

"It's happened. How's Ace?"

"Holding his own." My hound, rescued over a decade ago from South Carolina, had been prescribed three different medications by his vet. It never dampened his mood, based on things like his energy and appetite. Earlier in the day, I had rehomed a small cricket from the bathroom to the yard since I needed a break from thinking about the fact that living things die in the end.

Travis said, "What are you drinking?"

I pointed to his beer and said, "One of those. Do you want another?"

"No. My treat." He disappeared for a minute and then returned and handed me my own.

Up until that moment, I hadn't paid much attention to how people click bottles, sloppily, sometimes carelessly hitting the tapering section of the neck. Travis lined up our beers, pressed his against mine and held it there, smiling and blushing, and said, "Cheers then."

"Cheers."

He said, "I'm glad you came."

It tasted good. An IPA that soothed the throat and hinted at the final days of summer. The stronger smell of men's cologne brought me back into the room. I raked my left hand through my gelled hair and he grabbed my wrist on its way down. "A bracelet?"

"A present."

He said, "From an old flame?"

"No comment." Then I amended that with, "But just a flicker if that happened to be the case."

He chuckled.

I said, "Do you have your own place?"

"I rent a room from a guy who slipped off a roof while doing a home inspection. His brother has to bring him groceries now."

"Oh man."

"Oxy."

We drank while the crowd got gayer and the music got louder, both of us moving subtly to the pulsing sound in the background. It reached a point where the only way we could talk was by shouting. I grew restless and motioned toward the door with my empty beer bottle.

He said, "Inviting me over?"

"We never even had dinner together."

"You asked for one of the most mediocre plumbers in the whole company how many times and you expect me to believe you're still making up your mind?"

"Fine. But you owe me a real date someday."

The next morning, we walked around my neighborhood of six-week-high lawns and ominous oak trees. A leaf raker raised his gloved hand to us. I technically rented my parents' place and tended not to engage but Travis waved and smiled for both of us. At some point, I would find a neighborhood of my own choosing, with younger houses, conifers, and carpets of pine needles.

Ace trailed behind us at first but then I hefted him into my arms. When I got winded in a hilly section, Travis spelled me. He told me he dreamed of a vacation horseback riding around the Ring of Kerry in southwestern Ireland. I didn't see that coming at all. My own travel fantasy, that I didn't share, involved a cabin on the Big

Island doing a jigsaw puzzle with him at a more settled point in time. He stayed for dinner and, even after all that, I struggled with saying goodnight.

The following Friday he showed up at my door late with glassy, bloodshot eyes.

"I thought we said tomorrow."

He said, "I missed you."

"Come in then."

He wasn't flirting with unconsciousness or anything but I still tapped a few questions about alcohol poisoning into my phone. His skin temperature and breathing seemed unremarkable, so I fetched some water and loosened his clothes. He sat on the couch and covered his eyes with his hand.

"I went out with some friends. Had too many."

"Yeah. I guessed that part. Do you remember how many?"

"A bottle of wine is my limit."

"You were drinking wine?"

"No."

I sat up all night in an Eames chair, my mood darkening thinking about him driving to my house in that condition. My side of the bed called out to me a few times but the welter of a bucket, a damp washcloth on a garbage bag, a towel, and a cup of water disabused me of that idea. The next morning, I added aspirin, toast, and coffee on a tray.

He said, "My head hurts. Can we not do this right now?"

"We're not doing anything. I'm being present."

I didn't get a straight answer on how much he had the night before even though disinhibition and drinking are closely linked. Then again, heavy drinkers notoriously underestimate anyway. I had a vague sense that this problem existed. But no matter how the offer is presented, the nature of the job is only discovered at your desk.

We settled into a routine of his spending weekends at my house. As many people do now, he drank in a steady and terrifying way. I picked him up sometimes from the bar where he met up with the guys, like an anxious suburban dad. Other times, I left him to sort it out on his own and kept my fingers crossed. Probably a lot of factors were keeping him back from the cliff, but it was anybody's guess for how long.

Then one Sunday, he moved in after his landlord had a brush with naloxone.

When I gave him a key, he said, "I appreciate you doing this for me, buddy."

"Maybe now you'll stop asking if you can borrow some sugar every time we drink coffee."

He cleared his throat. "It's called manners."

Once he established a foothold, he ran the ship like an overeager first mate. I became liberated from washing clothes, walking Ace, and planning which repairs to tackle. Unstructured time re-emerged in my life like a mirage of my childhood. I read a few classics of psychological fiction just because I could.

As his birthday approached, I tracked down a place near the beach where we could ride. My sister, Judy, drove down from Philly to watch Ace since she owed me a favor. She cornered Travis and gave him what I assumed was a pep talk but at a low volume. I could tell he liked her by how much he laughed. She signed the letters for "wow" to me behind his back as we departed with our bags.

That Saturday, we rode easygoing brown morgans on the Eastern Shore. His was relaxed and dignified and mine had twitchy ears. It felt peaceful to be with my dude, trotting across the sand, looking at a tanker paused on the hazy horizon. Six months had passed since our first night out at the Every and it seemed like a different amount of time, but I wasn't sure in which direction.

He stroked the mane of his horse. "Give them a break?"

"Your birthday. You call the shots."

"Did we pass a gray picket fence yet?"

"I'm only marginally better at boundaries than you are."

We dismounted and walked the horses side-by-side while he located our position using his phone. I fed them both apples that had been approved before we left the stable. We were instructed to turn around no farther than the high marsh grasses because the terrain becomes unpredictable. The image of accidentally drowning a couple of thousand-pound horses and later seeing words to that effect on my credit card statement made me smile. Travis caught my eye and smiled back. He swiped the back of his hand down my arm.

He said, "Have some fun later?"

"I'm all yours."

"What else do you want?"

I said, "For you to drink less."

"I meant this weekend."

He took both sets of reins and I followed at a distance, checking my phone. My other life hadn't made any new demands on me, and I wondered if therapists exaggerated the importance of being available all the time. My most challenging client at the time was struggling with a crippling fear of medical bills and his suddenly losing lock on reality seemed unlikely.

That evening, we drove to the restaurant I found in my web research. Travis's dream meal would have been pizza on the bed, but I needed a real date. Our waiter recommended the Icelandic cod and some fresh local vegetables in a way that suggested our own selections would have been received poorly in the kitchen. While the sun went down, Travis interlaced his fingers with mine on top of the table. I interpreted the gesture as signaling he wasn't reconsidering the whole project just because I brought up alcohol earlier.

In bed later, I said, "You had a good time?"

He said, "Best birthday ever. I love Black Forest cake."

"I know that."

"How?"

When you listen for a living, words either register or you quit and become a gym teacher. "One of the nights you violated your one bottle of wine limit, you requested it. I said if you stuck around past the Ace era, I would switch to chocolate cakes."

He shook his head.

"It's a therapist thing. I don't remember everything. Mostly sentences that begin with 'my parents used to…'"

He got quiet. Even though we lived together now, and were in bed on vacation in just our boxer briefs, delaying sex for a few more minutes tops, I wondered if it felt too intimate to him that I knew his cake preference.

He said, "I remember some stuff about you too."

"Go on."

"You speak to dogs and babies like they can understand if you use short sentences. You take junk mail really personally. And you never shave on Saturdays, except for that one time you met me at the Every. I would say more but I don't want to turn this into a competition."

"Probably wise."

The next morning, we ate bagels on one of the benches along the town's boardwalk. The silences between us took on different qualities that I categorized as: unbreakable, restorative, fraught, and other.

It seemed like the third one, and I kicked his foot. "Why did you choose me?"

"That's a great question."

I was frustrated by the dodge but impressed that he switched from content to process. It would be a hard question for any lay person to answer accurately. My tenacity in demanding the same plumber each time would have scared most people off but just as easily could have flattered him. In any case, he had discovered a clever pathway, maybe owing to a stronger need than mine.

The wind had picked up, and while I sipped my coffee, I thought about the future. For some people, too much ambiguity can be like a rock in your shoe you can't remove. And it makes no difference how well ordered the universe happens to be at the time. Some self-destructive processes are mysterious enough that they can frustrate and even humble skilled clinicians.

I said, "How long are you staying?"

"Until you kick me out."

"I'm not in a rush for you to go anywhere but it's tough watching you drink so much."

"Okay."

After years of treating people, I knew that relationships and addictions could both stake profound claims and which won out boiled down to the fine print.

Ace tapped his tail on the floor, stood, and shook off when I opened the front door to my house. He and Travis scrambled outside to work off the excitement of their reunion.

Judy said, "How was the weekend?"

"I confronted him about his troubling level of drinking. Otherwise, relaxing."

"From your descriptions, I didn't picture him so rugged."

"That he is. He'll complain about his many aches and pains when he gets to know you better."

She said, "You do know it's on him what happens."

"Maybe you should lecture me on the subject."

"I'm just saying."

"Being wanted has to count for something. I don't know why. But I agree with you."

From the Author

During the pandemic, Friday night alcohol consumption around the fire pit jumped the fence to all kinds of get-togethers, like spin classes and farmers' markets. I wondered under what circumstances a sober person would feel something other than boredom when surrounded by people getting drunk. The obvious answer was that he would be attracted to someone in the group. That was the starting point for "Threading Die."

I chose Wiley's profession so that he would have insight into addiction from the outset and not be intimidated or overwhelmed by it. And Travis's profession because Wiley might be attracted to someone who solves problems with his hands.

About the Author

Chris Paranicas is a native of the northeast who currently lives in Maryland. He has published both fiction and non-fiction. One of his stories involving LGBT characters recently appeared in Gargoyle Magazine. He is currently working on a longer fiction piece.

He appreciates content and writing advice from Hildie, Bill, Holly, Larry, Rob, and Joanne, and for this story: Petra, Eliza, Pleasant, Carollyne, and Belinda.

Bowled Over

by
Katie Kent

Bowled Over

Becky, you know I love you, right?"
I peered at Laura over the top of my sunglasses as we sat
out in her garden. "Okay, what do you want?"

She put her hand to her heart. "Can't I tell my best friend I
love her without having an ulterior motive?"

"No." I folded my arms. "Out with it."

She swirled her straw around her glass, her tanned skin
glistening in the heat. "Alright, you got me. So, Mandy has broken
her arm. Can you sub for her in the team for a bit?"

"Absolutely not," I said immediately. "You'll have to find
someone else."

"But you're the only one who can legally fill in and give us a
chance of winning," she whined. "Come on, I know you miss it.
And I miss bowling with you."

"We go bowling all the time." I took a slurp of my cool drink,
envying Laura's short hair as mine stuck to my back.

"You know what I mean. As part of a competitive team."

I rubbed my forehead. "You know I can't do this. I have Uni
homework, for a start."

"It's only a few hours. And I know this isn't about Uni. Look."
She sighed. "I know that Ayana hurt you. But that was six months
ago. You can't avoid her forever."

"Watch me."

"I could ask her not to bring Aaron. But don't you want to
show him how well you're doing without him?"

I bit my nail. "Well..."

Laura saw a chink of hope and took advantage of it. "Besides,
I could do with the moral support to deal with my arch-nemesis."

"I forgot about her."

"We're playing them tomorrow afternoon. We've still not
managed to beat them since she joined the team, even with the
handicap." She clenched her hands into fists. "I really want to wipe
that smug expression off her face."

I couldn't help laughing. "You shouldn't let her get to you like this. Alright, you win. But I can only promise you one game. If I hate it, you'll have to find someone else next time."

"That's fair. But you won't hate it, I'm sure of that."

I leaned back in my seat. "I can't wait to meet the infamous Codie."

"I don't know if I can do this," I said the next afternoon, outside the doors of Ten Pin, our local bowling alley.

"Of course you can. Anyway, you can't abandon us now. We'd have to forfeit the game. Imagine Codie's reaction to that. She'd rub her hands with glee if she could win without even breaking a sweat." Laura held the door open.

I took a deep breath. "Alright. Let's do this."

As we walked in, I saw Aaron and Ayana were already there, doing a joint routine on the dance machine. Something constricted in my chest as I watched him dance with her; that used to be *our* thing. They looked good together, I had to begrudgingly admit to myself. I could certainly see the appeal of Ayana's dark skin, hair and eyes, and Aaron had a happiness about him that I hadn't seen for the last couple of months of our relationship.

Laura put her hand on my shoulder. "You've got this," she said. "I wouldn't have asked you to join us if I didn't think you could handle it."

I wished I had her confidence. I watched Aaron and Ayana as they finished their routine, throwing their arms around each other. Then, Ayana caught sight of me and nudged Aaron with her elbow. He whispered something to her, and then they started to walk toward me.

"Hey, Becky." Ayana put her hands in her pockets and looked hesitantly at me. Last time I'd seen her, she'd had her tongue down Aaron's throat. She'd tried to call me a bunch of times, and sent me a few texts, but I'd deleted them all without even listening to or reading them, eventually blocking her number—he was supposed to be *my* boyfriend.

Aaron cleared his throat. "It's good to see you."

My mouth felt dry. "I wish I could say the same to you." He'd dyed his hair blond. It didn't suit him.

Ayana winced, but they didn't deserve my forgiveness.

"Look." Laura put one arm around me and the other around Ayana. "We need to be a team here."

"You need my scores," I said, shrugging out of her grip. "We don't all need to get on."

"Well, I tried." Ayana turned her back on me and walked away, hand in hand with Aaron.

"You could have been a bit nicer." Laura had a pained expression on her face.

I shrugged. "I told you I didn't want to come." It wasn't like I had any feelings left for Aaron, but the betrayal still hurt, and I wasn't going to let either of them off the hook that easily.

"I…" Laura began, but her attention was suddenly taken by something else. "Don't look now, but she-who-can't-be-named has just walked through the door."

I turned around—and had to stop my jaw hitting the floor. I'd heard many things about Codie over the past few months. 'Codie's arrogant.' 'Codie's smug.' 'Codie's a bitch.' Not once did Laura say, 'Codie's drop-dead gorgeous,' although Laura was straight, so I guess it wouldn't have crossed her mind even if she hadn't been so busy hating her.

Codie was wearing skinny black jeans, red high-top Converse, and a red and black plaid shirt, undone at the front, over a white vest top. Her long, dark hair had blonde highlights in it, and she wore that casual, carefree expression of someone who knew they were hot without even trying.

I felt a 'whoomph' in my chest. "I need to sit down."

"What's the matter?" Laura pressed her hand against my forehead. "You do feel a bit warm."

"I just need a minute." My legs felt like jelly, and I stumbled over to a table in the bar area.

She narrowed her eyebrows. "Is this all because of Aaron?"

"I guess." It would be far easier to let her think that my ex had got to me than to tell her the truth—that her arch-nemesis was giving me all kinds of feels.

"Don't look now," Laura whispered. "The ice queen is on her way over."

Codie strode right up to our table, and I felt like I was about to spontaneously combust. "Who's this?" She arched one perfectly manicured eyebrow, and I tried not to pass out. She was even more stunning up close.

"B…Becky," I managed to mumble.

"Mandy has broken her arm," Laura explained. "Becky's subbing for her."

"Right. Well, may the best team win." She winked at us and strode off.

I let out a breath, and Laura slapped me on the back. "Don't worry, she has that effect on me, too."

I very much doubt it…

I followed Laura and Ayana to the lanes. It looked like Aaron had gone home—a fact that made me feel half satisfied, but also half annoyed that he thought I couldn't stand to see him there. Codie and her teammates, Ella and Liv, were already set up in the next lane. I tried my best to ignore her, putting my handbag down on the floor and sitting next to Laura.

"Which position do you want to bowl in?" she asked.

I felt far too nervous—for more than one reason—to go first. "Last."

She wrote our names on the scorecard. "Codie always goes last, too."

I winced inside, but it was too late to change it now, and I knew I was stuck going opposite her for every frame in the game.

Laura and Ayana matched the other team with their first goes—one strike and one spare. Then it was my turn, and the nerves started rushing through my body as I got up from my seat.

"Good luck," Ayana called out, but I didn't acknowledge her comment.

Codie got up from her seat. Arriving at the ball return, we went to pick up the same ball at the same time, and our fingers brushed.

I removed mine immediately, electricity sparking my fingertips. "Sorry."

She shrugged. "You take it."

That was not what I was expecting, given the story Laura had told me about their first meeting, when Codie had apparently stolen the ball that she was reaching her hand toward. It had always sounded like a stupid reason to hate someone if you asked me, but tensions can run high in these games.

"It's okay," I croaked. "It's yours."

She shrugged again, picking the ball up and striding confidently to the lane. I couldn't take my eyes off her as she swung her arm back and then forward, propelling the ball directly down the centre of the lane. All the pins crashed to the floor.

"Yes!" Ella shouted. "Straight down the middle."

Codie smirked. "The only time you'll hear the word 'straight' associated with me." Her eyes were trained on me as she spoke.

I swallowed as my mind registered the meaning behind her words, filling my head with inappropriate thoughts like what her lips would taste like if I kissed her right now, up against the ball return. I shook my head, trying to stop the fantasy before it got any further.

"What are you waiting for, Becky?" Laura called.

"The ball." I gestured lamely to the ball return. As the ball Codie had just used popped back up again, I picked it up with both hands, feeling Codie's eyes on me. Desperately trying not to blush, I walked toward the line, swung the ball back and forward and then released it.

It rolled slowly to the left and plopped into the gutter.

Taking a deep breath, ignoring the groans behind me and the laughter from the other team (whether it was Codie or the others on her team, I wasn't sure), I shut my eyes for a few seconds, trying to focus on the game and not on the hot girl sat a few feet away from me. I kept my head down as I walked back toward the ball return, not wanting to meet anyone's eyes as I bowled my second ball.

This time, my aim was a lot better. Nine pins clattered down, leaving just a single one at the back on the left.

I walked back to my teammates, feeling slightly less embarrassed.

"Good save," Ayana said, but I continued to blank her.

"Don't let Codie get to you." Laura took a sip from her bottle of Diet Coke.

"You never told me she was gay." I sat down next to her, hoping my tone came across as casual.

"Didn't I? Well, it's not really that important. It's not like I'd set you two up or anything. I wouldn't wish that on my worst enemy. Oh, I forgot—*she's* my worst enemy."

I tried to laugh.

"Besides, she's a total player. I've lost count of the number of girls I've seen her all over."

"Oh, right."

She screwed her eyes up. "Becks, you haven't got a thing for her, have you? Because I wouldn't trust her as far as I could throw her. And I have often fantasised about throwing her down the alley."

"What? Don't be silly. I have better taste than that." I forced my mouth into what I hoped vaguely resembled a smile.

"That's what I thought. Thank God."

Ayana's eyes scrutinised my face, and I turned away, fumbling in my bag for my lip gloss. The last thing I needed was for her to work out that I had a crush on Codie.

The rest of the game continued in much the same way. I got a couple of spares, one 6, some 7s, 8s and 9s, but not a single strike, and Codie's bowling seemed almost effortless in comparison. Only once did she get anything less than a strike, and that was a spare. Clearly I was not having the same effect on her she was having on me, but that was hardly surprising. As if someone who looked like that would be interested in a tall, lanky girl with mousy-brown hair and glasses. Unfortunately, Codie's dynamite skills on the bowling alley only made me fall for her even harder, and it was a struggle for me to keep my mind from going into the gutter, just like the ball I'd bowled.

"Sorry," I said when the game had finished, with Codie's team the easy winners. "I guess I'm a bit rusty. I wish I hadn't decided to go last."

"It's okay." Laura patted me on the back. "There's two more games to go. You'll pick it up."

As Codie passed Laura on our way to switch lanes again, she purposely took a step to the right, barging into Laura.

"Ouch." Laura glared at her.

Codie smiled sweetly. "Sorry. Didn't see you there."

Ella and Liv sniggered. They never used to be this annoying back when I used to play against them, before Codie joined their team. I could understand Laura's hostility toward Codie, although Codie's mean streak did nothing to dampen my feelings for her.

"Are you sure you'd rather not just admit defeat now?" Liv asked. "Your sub seems to have forgotten how to bowl."

Codie elbowed Liv in the ribs, whispering something to her. Liv rolled her eyes. I was itching to know whether Codie was joining in the teasing or whether she was defending me, but given what I knew about her, my money was on the former.

"You just see her when she's warmed up. You know how sharp she was," Laura said.

"Emphasis on the *was*." Ella smirked.

"Oh, shut up." Laura turned her back on them and sat down.

In the second game, I kept my eyes trained on Laura and Ayana as they took their turns, trying to put the blinkers on when it was my turn, as if I'd put the bumpers up in the lane. I got a strike on my first go, breathing a sigh of relief.

"She's back!" Laura spoke loudly enough for the other team to hear, but I didn't dare turn my head to see their reactions because I knew that as soon as I saw Codie's face, I'd be distracted all over again. I needed to focus on the game.

I didn't even pay attention to how the other team was bowling, so it was somewhat of a surprise when I rolled my last ball, all the pins fell down, and Laura yelled, "Get in! We won!" When I looked at the scorecard, I saw that Codie had actually rolled *all* strikes this time, and had already taken her extra go, but with my improved scores and Laura and Ayana doing better than their other two players, we were already ahead of them even without the handicap, and that was before my extra turn.

"Congratulations."

I jumped, not realising Codie had moved right next to me. She held her hand out.

"Th…thanks," I managed to get out, hoping she wouldn't notice how sweaty my hand was when I shook hers.

She held my hand for longer than felt comfortable. When she'd finally dropped it, I wiped it on my jeans, then worried Codie might think I thought she was dirty or something.

"Gotta pee," I told Laura, dashing off in the direction of the toilets. Inside, I bolted the cubicle door behind me and sat on the lid of the toilet, my head in my hands, groaning. This was bad. No one had affected me like this since Aaron, and I didn't like the way it made me feel. I wanted to leave, but we had one more game to play. And there was no way I could talk to Laura about the flips my stomach was doing every time I laid eyes on her enemy. So, I gritted my teeth and walked out of the bathroom like I didn't have a care in the world.

Laura bowled a spare, whilst Ella only managed a 9.

"Your turn, Becks!" Laura called out when Ayana was on her way back from taking her turn.

I took a deep breath, strode up to the ball return…and came face to face with Codie.

"Hi," she said as she reached her hand toward a ball, giving me a quick wink.

I pulled my hand away just in time, and tried to summon up my earlier willpower to forget she was even there, but my body had other thoughts.

I swept up a ball in one decisive motion and bowled it down the alley before she even had a chance to take her turn. Five pins went down. As I turned to pick up my next ball Codie propelled hers down the lane. Another strike.

She stayed just behind her lane as I walked toward mine with the ball. I waited a few seconds, but it was obvious that she wasn't going to budge, so I said a quick prayer in my head and released the ball.

It veered off to the right, knocking down just one extra pin on its way into the gutter.

Codie skipped back off to join her teammates, who were giggling like a couple of schoolgirls.

They know. The realisation made me break out in a cold sweat. Codie winking at me, staying close to me while I bowled, and the giggling. They all knew the effect she was having on me, and they were taking advantage of it. She was purposely trying to distract me, to put me off my game. And it was working.

As I sat down, I balled my hands into fists. How dare they exploit my feelings like this. I wasn't some character in a video game to be manipulated for their own ends. Codie may have been the hottest girl I'd ever seen, but I'd be damned if I let her ruin my game.

"You okay?" Ayana asked.

"Fine." I gave her a thumbs up, hoping the expression on my face looked more like a smile than a grimace.

On my next turn I tried to tune Codie out as much as I could, putting the full force of my anger at her behaviour behind the ball, and was rewarded with a strike. Of course she got one too, and we just couldn't match them in this game. I did okay, but toward the end, the effort of trying to ignore the stunning girl next to me and concentrate on the game got to be too much, and my scores started to suffer again.

"I'm sorry," I told Laura after the game. "I know you wanted to beat them."

She shrugged. "There's always next time. There will be a next time, right?"

"Umm." I hesitated, but despite my anger toward Codie's behaviour, I had enjoyed being part of a team again, and if I was honest, part of me really wanted to see Codie again. "Yeah. And I promise I'll be better next time."

The next weekend, we were playing another team. I felt a lot calmer as I approached Ten Pin, knowing that Codie would not be there. We were playing on Sunday, and her game had been the day before. I didn't even care that Aaron was with us; I hadn't stopped thinking about Codie since our last game, and my thoughts were far away from my ex, although I wasn't about to let him and Ayana off the hook that easily.

"I don't believe it."

I'd just followed Laura through the doors, and walked into the back of her when she suddenly came to a stop.

"What is it?" I stepped next to her, following her line of sight, and felt my eyes widen. Codie and Ella stood next to the air hockey table. Codie was wearing a grey boob tube, showing off a tantalising amount of bare skin and a belly button piercing. I felt like my legs were going to give way.

"She's never watched us take on anyone else before." Laura frowned. "What's she playing at? And what the fuck is she wearing?"

"Probably trying to put us off our game," Ayana said with a quick glance at me.

I cleared my throat. "Let's get on with it then, shall we?" I strode right up to the lane, trying my best to ignore Codie as I said hi to our opponents, but just as we were about to start, I decided I needed to quickly pop to the toilet first.

When I came out of the cubicle, Codie was standing at one of the sinks, applying bright red lipstick while she looked in the mirror. Her eyes flicked in my direction in the mirror, and I found myself wishing I'd run the brush through my hair one more time before I'd left. She smacked her lips together, and I tried to do my best impression of someone whose body was not reacting to the scene happening next to her. But it *was* reacting. Hard.

"Alright?" Her eyes scrutinized my face.

I turned the tap on and rubbed my hands under the water. "Laura says you've never watched us play anyone else before."

"I have my reasons." She winked at me and walked away, leaving me standing there muttering to myself. It was clear what she was doing, but I was *not* going to let her do this to me two games in a row.

Luckily, the team we were playing were right at the bottom of the league, and we won the first game easily, despite the distraction sitting nearby.

Before the second game started Laura decided she wanted a snack, and I offered to go and get it. As I was about to turn the corner to the food counter, I heard familiar voices, and flattened myself against the wall.

"Can we leave now?" It was Ella.

"You promised we could stay until the end," Codie said.

Ella sighed. "Look, I don't care how cute you think this girl is. There are so many other things I could be doing rather than watching other teams play. Like studying. Or seeing my boyfriend."

"But—"

"You need to calm your libido down, mate. What's got into you? God help you if you ever see her in a skirt, with your thing for legs."

A smile broke out upon my face. It was somewhat of a surprise that Codie was into me, too—I'd thought her way out of my league—but I could use this as payback. She'd used my attraction to her to put me off my bowling, and two could play that game.

I played a lot better for the rest of our match, buoyed up with this new knowledge and already planning my revenge. We destroyed the other team.

The next weekend's game was uneventful. There was no sign of Codie, and I got into my stride quickly. We were easy victors.

"That was great," Laura said as we were packing away after the game. "But you know what comes next. We need to beat Codie and her crew next weekend to have a shot at the league title."

"We will. I can sense it."

Ayana looked at me suspiciously. "You're confident."

I just shrugged. "Why wouldn't I be?"

As I got ready the next weekend, I couldn't help smiling. Aaron had always said I had nice legs, and after the comment I'd overheard about Codie's inclinations, I'd known exactly what to wear for the next match.

Laura sighed as she looked me up and down after getting out of her car on my driveway, her eyes taking in my mini skirt and bare legs. "Please tell me you're not wearing that for Aaron."

I hadn't even stopped to consider how it would look when I turned up in an outfit my ex always said he loved to see me in. "I'm not, I promise."

"I thought you were over him," she said.

"I am. I just wanted to look good, that's all. I assure you that this has nothing at all to do with Aaron. Hand on heart. I'm over him." *And under someone else...*

She shook her head. "Whatever. I just hope this doesn't make things awkward with Ayana."

"If things are awkward, she only has herself to blame." I opened the passenger door. "She's the one who stole my boyfriend, after all."

"Becks…" she began, but I just hopped into the car, shutting the door behind me.

We drove in silence, but when we were almost there, she tried again. "You know you can talk to me about anything, right?"

Anything but my crush on your arch-nemesis. "I'm good." I put my hand over hers on the wheel. "Don't worry about me."

Codie and her team were already there when we arrived, setting up in the lane. She was wearing the same boob tube as last time, and there were waves in her hair. My mouth watered, but I needed to stay composed this time.

"Hi," I said, leaning casually against the glass that separated our lanes.

When she looked up, her eyes looked like they were about to pop out of her head. "Hey." I liked how hard she was trying not to check my legs out and the blush that appeared on her cheeks as she fought to keep up her persona of the ice queen, the machine, the one who was always in charge. *Not this time, girl.*

Ayana and Aaron arrived, hand in hand. His eyes went straight to my legs, but not in the way Codie's eyes had. He whispered something to Ayana.

"I don't think this is for you," I heard her say back to him, and I had to hide a smile.

"Which position do you want to bowl in this time?" Laura asked.

I peered through the screen to the other team's scorecard. "Last."

"You sure?"

"Positive."

Laura and Ayana started off well, scoring higher than Ella and Liv.

Codie and I strode up to our lanes at the same time. I winked at her and then propelled the ball right down the middle of the lane, scoring a strike.

At the same time, she got a 9, and as I looked into her eyes, I saw uncertainty in them for the first time. With me watching, her second ball missed the last pin by inches.

"Fuck," she muttered, and it was my turn to smirk.

"Distracted by something?" I asked.

She just shook her head, her face turning red.

"Maybe keep your eyes on your lane next time." I walked off before she had a chance to reply.

On her next turn she could only manage to knock down six pins, whilst I got another strike.

"Will you just fucking get your head in the game?" I heard Liv ask her as she sloped back off to her seat, and I smiled to myself.

I had to say, the knowledge of the effect I was having on her was really turning me on too, but I couldn't let myself get distracted again. I had a job to do here, and I needed to be the one in control.

"I've never seen her have a bad game before," Laura said after our third goes. This time I'd got a spare, and Codie had only managed eight. "I wonder what's got into her."

I tried to keep a straight face. "No idea."

We won the first game, and Laura punched the air with delight.

"We've still got to win another two games. And she might be less distracted this time," Ayana said with a sideways look at me.

I just gave her my most innocent expression back, like I didn't have a clue what she was talking about. She'd clearly cottoned onto what was happening, but whether she knew the full story, I wasn't sure. I just hoped she wouldn't say anything to Laura, although it wasn't like anything had happened beyond a bit of harmless flirting.

It turned out that Codie was *not* less distracted the second time.

"Alright?" I asked her as we both approached the ball return.

"I'm good." I could tell she was trying to be cool, but the croak in her voice gave her away.

I watched as she reached for the ball, making sure to stick my hand out at the exact same time. As our fingers touched, she pulled hers away as if she'd been shocked with electricity. I felt goosepimples all over my arm and had to have words with myself in my head. I could *not* let her gain the upper hand again.

"You take it." I gestured toward the ball with my head.

She didn't reply, just picked the ball and strode up to the lane. I had to stifle a laugh when I saw her hold the ball up to her face, shut her eyes and mumble something.

"Praying you'll keep your mind on the shot this time?" I asked.

She opened her eyes. "Whatever." She stepped back and bowled the ball down the alley. It veered off to the left, taking four pins with it.

My glee gave me added impetus, and all the pins clattered down with my first shot. Codie looked at me, her eyes blazing.

I stepped closer and whispered in her ear. "Don't you like it when you're not in control?"

She swallowed, and from the look she gave me, I could tell how fast her heart was racing. Mine wasn't far behind, to be honest.

"Better take your shot." I made no attempt to move farther away from her, even though it was taking every single ounce of self-control I had not to lean my head toward hers and kiss her.

She released the ball, and once again it went off to the left, only knocking down another two pins.

"You seem to have lost your ability to play it straight," I said quietly, then went back to my seat.

"What were you and the ice queen talking about?" Laura asked, as Ayana headed toward the lane.

"Oh, I was just psyching her out." I took a swig of Dr Pepper from my bottle; Codie wasn't the only one who needed cooling down.

"Well, it seems to be working. Keep it up."

We won the second and third games too, and Codie, Ella, and Liv had faces like thunder as we all packed up afterward.

"Better luck next time." Laura couldn't keep the smile off her face.

Codie just charged through the doors, not stopping to look behind her.

"We finally beat them!" Laura gave me a high five. "You were on fire! Did you see the look in Codie's eyes? It looked like she was about to have an aneurism."

I was more taken by the pure lust in her eyes, but clearly I couldn't tell Laura that.

The next Friday night, we had the league's annual mid-season party at a local hotel. My heart was thumping as we approached the doors. Without a game to play, without a focus, I doubted my abilities to resist Codie if she came onto me.

I had dressed in another skirt, with a flowery blouse. Walking into the hotel, my eyes sought Codie out immediately. She was wearing a black leather jacket over a low-cut red top, with white skinny jeans. As her eyes found mine, my gaze was drawn to the smoky makeup around her eyes and her bright red lipstick. We held each other's gaze more than was normal for two casual acquaintances.

"Let's get a drink." Laura took my hand and pulled me to the bar, straight past Codie and her friends.

Codie sprung up immediately, standing right next to me. "Can I get you two ladies a drink?"

"We're not playing tonight, Codie," Laura said. "You don't need to psyche us out."

"I was just trying to be nice."

Laura burst into laughter. "Yeah, right. You wouldn't know nice if it jumped up and bit you on the ass."

"Suit yourself." She turned to me. "What about you, Becky?"

My mouth had gone dry. "I'm good, thanks." I didn't want to risk provoking Laura's suspicion by accepting a drink from the person I knew she hated.

"See you later, then." Her arm brushed mine as she left, and I had to force myself not to shiver. I knew the implication behind that 'later.'

"Can you believe her?" Laura said.

"Maybe she's trying to turn over a new leaf."

"Yeah, right." Laura laughed. "Once a bitch, always a bitch. She doesn't have a nice bone in her body."

We ordered our drinks and carried them over to Aaron and Ayana, who were already sat at a table.

"What did Codie want?" Ayana asked, as we took our seats.

"Apparently she wanted to buy us drinks." Laura rolled her eyes. "She was probably planning to spit in them or something."

Ayana took a swig of her drink. "Don't you think it's about time you ended this feud of yours?"

"When Hell freezes over. I wonder how many girls we'll see her all over this evening." She pulled a face.

Just me, I hope. I tried to shake the thought from my head, but it seemed somewhat inevitable.

About an hour later, I excused myself for a toilet visit. Codie and I hadn't spoken again since that initial encounter at the bar, but I couldn't help but notice the frequent glances she aimed my way, and I was no better—I could barely take my eyes off her. I hoped the others would take my odd mumbles throughout their conversations for me paying attention, but I didn't really have a clue what they were talking about.

After using the toilet, I walked to the sink, turned on the tap and scrutinized myself in the mirror as I washed my hands. I was the only person in there, and I splashed cold water on my face, trying to cool myself down.

Drying my hands and throwing the paper towel into the wastebasket, I turned around—and almost walked straight into Codie. The look she gave me left me in no doubt as to what was on her mind. She grabbed my hand and pulled me into a cubicle, bolting it behind us, then lunged at me—but I pulled my head away at the last minute.

"You're driving me crazy." Codie licked her lips, and I could feel the sexual tension buzzing around us. "Look, I know you're into me. So why are you resisting?" Her voice was croaky.

I shifted my body slightly back, knowing I was teetering on the edge of the abyss. Just a step forward, and there would be no way back. The fantasy filled me with adrenaline. "My best friend can't stand you."

"Eh." Codie shrugged. "It's not her I'm trying to date."

"You wanna date me?" My voice was squeaky.

She rolled her eyes. "Well, duh. Have I not made that obvious already?"

"Laura says you're a player."

This time, Codie sighed. "Laura just sees what she wants to see. If she took the time to know me, she'd know that I'm not really like that."

"Then why do you antagonise her?"

She leaned back against the wall. "I dunno, really. It's just a way to pass the time, I guess. She's easy to wind up."

"And what about all the winding up you've been doing of me? Trying to put me off the game and stuff."

"Oh, come on. It's not like I'm the only one, is it? You hit back as good as I gave. I've never lost a game before. I was so distracted I barely even remembered how to throw a ball." She leaned closer and whispered in my ear. "Yours were the only pins on my mind that day."

I shivered, feeling a smile flit across my face. "I almost lost it when I saw you in that boob tube. It's a good job we were playing a team that wasn't that good."

She grinned. "Touché. So, we've established that we both fancy the pants off each other. Ball's in your lane now."

"What about all the girls Laura's seen you with?" I watched her face as I asked the question.

"There haven't been that many. She's exaggerating."

"How many?" I probed.

"It's not like I've been counting. Does it really bother you that much?" She shook her head. "Look, if you must know, I was burned about a year ago. I was totally in love with this girl, and then I found out that she was cheating on me. So, I've tried hard not to catch feelings for anyone else, in case I get hurt again. But I really like you. And I'm being serious. This is me letting my guard down. I haven't seen any other girls since I met you. I want you. Bad. And I know you want me, too."

"I know what it's like to be cheated on," I said quietly. "I get how it can mess with your head."

"So you believe me?"

"I guess I do."

She suddenly stepped forward, pushing a lock of hair out of my face and tucking it behind my ear. "Don't fight this, Becky."

And I couldn't—not anymore. Tilting my head forward, my lips met hers, and then we were all over each other. I kissed her like we were running out of time. Her lips were soft and warm, and I couldn't get enough of them. I'd known I was bi for ages, but I'd been with Aaron for so long that I'd never even kissed a girl before.

It was different than kissing him; softer yet somehow more passionate, almost.

Then we heard the door to the toilets open and sprung apart. I put my finger to my lips as Codie clambered up onto the toilet seat. Once we'd heard the person leave, I breathed a sigh of relief.

"I should probably be getting back. Before Laura comes to find me," I said.

She jumped down off the seat. "How do you think she'll take this?"

"We can't tell her."

She frowned. "You want to keep me a secret?"

"Just for now." I reached out for her hand. "You know how she feels about you. I just need to find the right time to tell her about us."

She lifted my hand to her lips and kissed it. "Alright. But it's going to be hard to keep my hands off you next time we play each other."

"You won't need to." I leaned closer, whispering in her ear. "When I go to the toilet, just follow me."

She grinned. "You might want to wipe your face before you go back. You've got my lipstick all over it."

After wiping off her lipstick, I strode casually back to the table and sat down next to Laura, who was now sat there alone, messing about with her phone.

"You okay?" she asked, setting her phone down on the table. "You were gone ages."

"Time of the month," I lied. "Where are the others?"

Her eyes drifted to the right, and I followed her line of sight. Aaron and Ayana were on the dance floor. He had his hands on her bum as she wrapped hers around his neck.

"Oh, right." I downed the rest of my drink, wishing it didn't still hurt to see them together. My feelings for him were no longer there, and I was buzzing with adrenaline from the encounter with Codie, but the moment I had discovered their betrayal still played over and over in my mind.

"I'm sorry, mate."

I waved her concern off. "I'm fine." I watched as Codie and her friends arrived on the dance floor. "Let's go and dance."

Laura narrowed her eyes. "Are you sure?"

"Yeah." I grabbed her hand and pulled her to her feet.

On the dance floor, I manoeuvred myself so I stood as close to Codie as I could without raising suspicion, watching her out of the corner of my eye as I twisted myself around to the beat. I'd always been a good dancer, and I could almost feel the heat coming off her as I moved.

"You tease," she whispered to me as my hair flicked across her face.

I was sleeping off my hangover the next morning when my phone started to ring.

"Ugh." I pulled my pillow over my ears, letting the phone go to voicemail, but a few seconds later it started to ring again. Groaning, I picked it up. I didn't recognise the number, so I pressed the button to end the call. Seconds later, it started up again.

I picked up the phone, barking, "Who is this?" into the receiver.

"It's me. The ice queen."

Just like that, my bad mood evaporated. "Hey, you. How'd you get my number?"

"I have my ways." Her voice was like a tonic. "You okay? You sounded grumpy when you answered the phone."

"Hangover," I told her. "My head feels like it's in a vice. How the hell are you so breezy?"

She laughed. "I don't drink. I was on soft drinks all night."

"Oh, right."

"Hang on." Her tone suddenly became serious. "You do remember last night, right?"

"Of course." I lay back against my pillow, the pain in my head replaced with lust. "You think I could forget how your lips felt against mine? I wish you were here right now."

"That can be arranged. Give me your address, and I'll be right over."

"You wanna go on a date with me?" Codie asked, later, as we lay next to each other in my bed. I hadn't expected us to jump into bed with each other quite so soon, but as soon as she got to my room, we were ripping each other's clothes off. It just felt right, and I had zero regrets.

"Right now, I want to spend the rest of my life in bed with you," I said, running my fingers up and down her thigh.

She shivered. "Well, me too, but we should go on a proper date, don't you think? I want to buy you dinner."

I giggled. "Careful; you could be in danger of losing your ice queen label."

She raised her eyebrows. "Well, if anyone can heat me up, it's definitely you."

"What about all those girls Laura saw you with?"

She propped herself up on one elbow. "I thought we'd got over all that. I told you, it was all an act. I didn't want to get close to anyone."

"So you used them all."

She drew her knees up to her chin. "If you want to dress it up like that. Okay, so perhaps I *was* a player. But it wasn't really me. Look, I'm not proud of the way I acted. But they all knew the deal. I only ever saw any girl once, so it wasn't like she could get too attached. I didn't leave a trail of broken hearts behind me, or anything. People were aware of my reputation."

"How do I know you're not going to do the same to me? How do I know you're not going to sleep with me and then discard me?"

She sighed. "Becks, I never slept with any of those girls." She traced her finger around my nipple, causing fresh waves of lust to ripple through me. "If I was trying not to get too close to anyone, I could never have given myself to them like that. If you were just another one of them, I wouldn't be here naked in your bed, and I definitely wouldn't have just asked you out on a date."

I blinked at her. "But Laura said—"

"That I was all over them," she interrupted. "I know. And yeah, she wasn't wrong. I made out with a *lot* of girls. But that's where it ended. I mean, where did you think I got the name 'ice queen' from? They all thought they'd be the one to warm me up." A tear slid out of her eye and made its way down her cheek, and she rubbed it away. "I just gave you my virginity. Trust me, that's a big deal to me. My ex, she really did a number on me."

My eyes went wide. "That was your first time?"

She laughed. "Yeah. Don't tell anyone; it would ruin my reputation." Her face became serious. "I hope it was adequate."

"You idiot." I swatted her with my hand. "It was more than adequate." Aaron and I had slept together more than a few times, but this was my first time with a girl.

"Good to know." She jumped on top of me. "Because I plan on doing a lot more of that."

Codie and I arranged our first date for that evening, after our next games. As we packed away after our game, which we'd won, Laura asked me, "Do you want to hang out tonight? Apart from bowling, I feel like I've barely seen you lately, what with Uni and everything."

"I can't, sorry." I picked my bag up. "I've got something else on."

"What?" She pulled on her coat.

"Oh, just a family thing," I said vaguely. "Uncle's birthday."

"Well, maybe next time."

"That would be nice." I did miss hanging out with Laura, but it was her attitude toward Codie that meant I had to keep this from her.

"Have fun."

"I will." I had to force my face not to break out into a grin.

I felt like my heart was going to stop when Codie came to pick me up that evening. Dressed in a black shoulderless top and her white jeans with her hair straightened, my insides did funny things when I looked at her.

She looked me up and down in my black and white polka dot dress. "You look amazing. Sorry, I don't really do dresses."

"You're fine as you are. Trust me."

Her smile lit up her whole face. "Well, I've got the car, and I've booked us a table at an Italian restaurant about half an hour's drive away. Just so we don't run into Laura or anything."

"Thanks," I said. "I know I'm going to have to tell her eventually. I just need to work up to it. She thinks you're the devil incarnate."

She smirked. "I can be a devil if you want me to."

I pulled her toward me, kissing her briefly. "Not right now, or we'll never make it to dinner."

Sitting opposite each other at the table, I couldn't take my eyes off Codie as she ran her finger down the menu.

She looked up. "What?"

"I was just thinking how gorgeous you are, and how lucky I am."

"I'm the lucky one. After Brogan, I never thought..." She shook her head. "I didn't think I could be this happy again."

The date went well—we chatted away as if we'd known each other for years, and she insisted on paying for everything. She was so far away from the ice queen, player, and bitch that Laura thought she was.

In the car on the way home, she was a lot quieter, and I could tell that there was something on her mind.

"Are you nervous?" I teased her when we pulled onto my driveway.

Codie tapped the steering wheel with her fingers. "Is it that obvious? Look, I wanted to ask you if you'll be my girlfriend. Officially, I mean."

"As if I'd say no." I leant across and kissed her, slowly. "I really like you, in case you hadn't figured that out already."

She smiled. "Well, I really like you, too."

"I'm still not ready to tell Laura yet," I said. "I'm sorry. I know it's not really fair to keep you hidden like this."

She nodded. "I get it. I'm sure she won't be impressed when she finds out. I'm not her favourite person, after all."

"I think Ayana knows." I linked my fingers with Codie's. "At least, she's picked up on the chemistry between us."

She raised her eyebrows. "Chemistry, hey?"

"Let me show you some of that chemistry." I climbed over to her side of the car, squeezing between her and the steering wheel, and straddled her, my head facing hers.

She moaned. "What are you trying to do to me, girl?"

The next time we played Codie's team, it was obvious to me that she was trying to make an effort with Laura.

"Good luck." She stuck her hand out.

Unfortunately, Laura just laughed. "Yeah, right. You know we beat you last time?" Laura made no effort to shake Codie's hand, so Codie just let it fall awkwardly to her side.

Sorry, I mouthed to Codie, but she just shrugged.

The first game was close, but I was back to my best, and we won by a single point.

As we were about to start the second game, I caught Codie's eye, and the look she gave me back almost made me collapse on the floor.

"Just gotta pee first," I announced, loudly, enjoying the smile that flicked across her face.

Standing next to the sinks, I didn't have to wait long before Codie came through the door. She didn't say anything, just put her hand on my chest and pushed me backward into one of the cubicles. After locking the door, she pounced on me, kissing me hard, her hands roaming all over my body. I lost all track of time as I kissed her back, thoughts of bowling forgotten for the moment.

"I've been wanting to do that all afternoon," she said breathlessly.

"Me too." I tipped her head back toward mine.

"We should probably head back before they get suspicious."

I shushed her with a finger across her lips. "Soon."

She laughed. "Someone's thirsty."

"I am *so* thirsty," I said, watching her pupils dilate as she leaned back toward me, beginning round two.

"Ahem."

I pulled away from Codie, turning my head to see the door open and Ayana standing in front of us, eyebrows raised. "Well, this is interesting."

"It's not what it looks like." I couldn't meet Codie's eyes as I spoke.

"What, so you were just tasting each other's lip gloss to see which was better?"

"Shit." I bit my lip. "Okay, you got me. It was totally what it looked like."

"I'll leave you two alone." Codie touched me lightly on the shoulder as she left, leaving Ayana and me in there alone. I pushed the toilet lid down and sat on it, my head in my hands. My body was still filled with adrenaline from the kiss.

Ayana's voice boomed in my ears. "I take it Laura doesn't know about this?"

I raised my head. "No."

"I don't think she'll be very impressed."

I stood up. "You can't tell her. I'm begging you, Ayana."

"Was that a one-time thing?" she asked. "Or has it happened before?"

I scratched the top of my head. "She's my girlfriend, I guess."

Ayana just stared at me. "Since when?"

"A few weeks."

She shook her head. "You're playing with fire."

"I really like her." My voice wavered.

"Well, that much was obvious from the way you were going at her."

I felt my cheeks burn.

"It's not like it's that much of a surprise," Ayana said. "It's pretty obvious that you've had the hots for her ever since the first time you met. And I knew what was behind your outfit the last time we played them. She couldn't take her eyes off your legs. Nice bit of distraction there. But I wasn't sure if anything had actually happened between you two."

"We got together at the party. You probably didn't notice because you were all over Aaron on the dance floor."

She winced, but before she could say anything back, I added, "I did try to resist her—I know Laura's feelings toward her—but I just couldn't. She's shit hot and the tension between us had already gotten too much. I don't think we could have kept that game up for much longer."

"Look, I won't say anything," Ayana said, and relief rushed through me. "But I think *you* should. Laura's bound to find out sooner or later anyway, if you're planning to keep seeing Codie."

I just looked down at the floor. There was no question that I was going to keep seeing Codie.

"It's kind of weird that I would be the one to find you two, don't you think? After you found me and Aaron that time."

I swallowed. "It's hardly the same, is it? Codie isn't dating one of my friends. Anyway, we don't have to talk about that now." I hadn't ignored all those calls and texts from her for no good reason. I didn't think there would ever be a good time to talk about this.

She folded her arms, leaning back against the doorjamb. "Well, now is as good a time as any. It's not like I haven't tried before."

I sighed, resigning myself to the conversation I'd never wanted to have. "I thought we were friends. So why did you do it?"

There was a haunted expression on her face. "It just kind of happened. It's not like either of us meant for it to. I hated that you found out like that."

"It would have hurt no matter how I found out."

"I know." She rubbed her eyes. "And I don't know how many times I can say I'm sorry. But I fell for him, just like the way you've fallen for Codie. Love isn't always rational. I hated that it was him that I felt like that about. If it was just one-sided, I would have stepped back, of course. I would have left the team, removed myself from that situation. But it wasn't. The first time we kissed, we tried to avoid each other for a bit, but when we eventually got together to talk about it, neither of us could deny what was happening between us. We agreed to tell you straight away, but it was so hard. Neither of us wanted to be the one to break your heart. I know we should have been honest with you, but it wasn't that easy. We didn't want to hurt you."

I kept quiet, digesting her words.

"I miss your friendship," she said, and I could tell she meant it.

I stood up and threw my arms around her. It took her a second to respond, but then I felt her hugging me back.

"Now, are you absolutely sure about Codie?" she asked, when we'd both pulled back. "In your head as well as your heart. She hasn't exactly got the best reputation, after all."

"I'm sure. I haven't felt like this about anyone since Aaron. And she's not a bad person." I traced a shape on the floor with my right foot.

"I'd hate to think she was using you."

"She's not," I said immediately. "At least, I don't think she is."

"Well, I haven't seen her with anyone else since you guys met," she conceded. "So hopefully you're right. But you still need to tell Laura. You can't keep it hidden forever. Especially not if you're planning on snogging her in the toilets at every opportunity you get. You and I both know how easily secrets like that can get out, and how important honesty can be when it comes to situations like this."

"You're right." I fiddled with the ring on my finger. "I'll tell her after the game."

Codie's team won the game, but it was close. As everyone was packing up, I cornered Laura.

"Laura." The nerves were bubbling up inside my stomach, making me feel like I was about to throw up. "There's something I need to tell you."

"Alright." She gave me a puzzled look. "What is it? You look really serious."

"Me and Codie, we're…" I shot Codie a look, but she had her head down, doing up her shoelaces. Even just looking at the back of her head filled me with a warm, fuzzy feeling. "We're dating."

"No way. This is a joke, right?"

I just shook my head. "I've been into her from the start. We got together at the party, and now she's my girlfriend. I was just afraid to tell you."

She sat down on one of the seats. "Why does it have to be her? Your taste sucks, mate."

"I think it's time you two ended your grudge," I said. "She's willing to. You just need to give her the benefit of the doubt."

"Look, even I can see how objectively 'hot' she is," Laura said, doing air quotes with her fingers. "But it's what's inside that counts."

"You don't even know her."

"And you do?" she shot back. "Just because you've swapped spit with her, doesn't mean you know how her mind works."

"Eww. Anyway, it's more than that. I think I'm falling for her."

Laura groaned. "Becky, don't go mistaking a rebound thing for love."

"This isn't a rebound thing." I clenched my fists as my voice rose. "This has nothing to do with Aaron. I'm really into this girl. How are you not getting that?"

"She'll only break your heart."

"Whatever. I'm willing to take that chance." I forced myself to take a deep breath, rather than blow up further. "I knew you'd react like this. That's why I kept it hidden from you. Do you know how hard it was to keep my feelings from my best friend? I could have done with the support, but I knew you wouldn't understand. I'm sorry I wasn't honest from the start. I've learned from Ayana where hiding things can lead to."

"Please tell me you haven't slept with her," was all she said in reply.

When I felt a blush spread across my cheeks, she groaned again. "You know that was probably all she was after. This is what she does—fucks a girl and then moves onto the next one."

"Actually," I said, "I was her first time."

She laughed. "Yeah, right. As if little miss slut was a virgin. I can't believe the lies she's been feeding you. You really are under her spell, aren't you? Look, I'm just trying to protect you."

I shook my head, feeling the anger surface again. "Where was this indignation when I caught Ayana with her tongue down my boyfriend's throat? You didn't even say anything to her. In fact, it was as if…" I trailed off as a thought wormed its way into my brain. "You knew, didn't you?"

She didn't say anything, just chewed her thumbnail, which she always did when she was nervous about something.

"I can't believe this." I turned to walk away from her.

She reached out and grabbed my shoulder. "Becks—"

"Save it." I shrugged my shoulder away from her hand. "You're happy to tell me how Codie is no good for me and claim that you're trying to protect me, but you never even told me that my boyfriend was cheating on me with my friend."

Codie looked over when I raised my voice, and she must have seen me wipe the tears away from my eyes as she was immediately by my side. "Everything okay?" She looked from me to Laura, and then back to me again.

"Not really." I reached out for her hand and gave it a squeeze. "Can you please take me home?"

"Of course." She turned back to her teammates. "See you guys later."

I followed her out to her car. She held the door open for me, and I climbed into the passenger seat.

"This isn't just about me, is it?" she asked, when we'd both done our seatbelts up. "I'm assuming you told her about us. She was looking at me like she wanted to kill me, even more than usual."

"Partly." I sighed. "She thinks you're no good for me. But not completely, no."

"I'm not going to pry," she said. "But if you want to talk…"

My eyes filled with tears. Codie undid her belt and leaned across, cradling my head against her chest. Then it all came out— everything with Aaron and Ayana, the fact that I'd found them snogging during that game, the fact I'd walked out and we'd had to forfeit the game, and the fact that apparently Laura had known all along.

Codie reached across to the glove compartment, pulled out a pack of tissues and handed one to me. "Not that I'm keen to defend someone who thinks I'm no good for you," she said as I blew my nose, "but she probably just didn't know how to tell you. Maybe you should hear her out."

I smiled through my tears. "She's got it so wrong about you. She's so caught up in this feud that she can't even face the idea that there might be more to the girl that I love than the idea she has of you in her head."

"You love me?"

I felt my face turn red. "I didn't mean to say that," I mumbled. "I mean, I know we've only been dating for a few weeks. I didn't mean to scare you off or anything—"

She cut me off by leaning toward me and planting a kiss on my lips. "You didn't scare me," she said once she'd pulled away. "I kinda love you, too."

"You do?"

"Yeah." She bopped me on the nose with her finger. "I think I've loved you from the first time I saw you, if I'm honest."

"Really? I thought you were way out of my league."

She burst into laughter. "That was just my 'ice queen' persona."

I grinned. "The fact you were smoking hot may have had something to do with it. But yeah, you seemed so cool and aloof the first time I met you."

She twirled a lock of hair around her finger. "It was all just an act. Inside, I was bricking it, wondering how on earth I was going to concentrate on the game with such a cute girl distracting me."

"You seemed to manage okay that first time." I stuck out my tongue. "Me, on the other hand…" I flung my fingers out in a 'boom' gesture.

She reached out and entwined my fingers with hers. "I have to admit, it was fun teasing you like that. But the more time I spent around you, the harder you were to ignore. It became less about the game and more about you. And anyone who knows me knows that bowling is my life. Since Brogan dumped me, girls were just a way to pass the time. At least until I met you."

Laura tried to call me several times over the next week, but I didn't answer any of them, and I deleted all her voicemails and texts. My silent feud with her had to come to a head eventually, however, because we had a game the next weekend. As I approached the doors of Ten Pin, I saw Laura's car in the car park and my legs started to shake, but Codie squeezed my hand, and I felt my courage come back.

"Are you sure you want me to come in with you?" she asked. "I don't want to make things worse."

"I'm sure. You're my girlfriend. You belong at my side."

She kissed me on the cheek, and then stepped in front of me, holding the door open.

Laura and Ayana were stood to the side, chatting, as we walked in. There was no sign of Aaron. When she saw me, Ayana elbowed Laura in the ribs, and they both fell silent.

"I tried to call you," Laura said as we approached them. "Several times. I texted, too."

"I know. I've been busy. With my *girlfriend*." I put emphasis on the last word.

"I'm just gonna get a drink." Codie turned to leave but I pulled her back to me, kissing her right on the lips. Let Laura witness our PDA.

"I'll join you," Ayana said, once we'd pulled apart.

They walked off together, leaving me and Laura facing each other.

"Ayana said she could spot the chemistry between you two from a mile off." Laura chewed her thumbnail. "I guess I was too busy hating Codie to notice." She sighed. "I'm sorry you felt like you couldn't share this with me."

"It was tough, to be honest," I admitted. "I mean, I knew that Codie was your enemy and that I was supposed to hate her. But when I first met her, all I could think was how hot she was. It did mess with my head. But I guess I understand now why it was difficult for you to tell me about Aaron and Ayana."

"Yeah. I didn't want to keep such a big secret from you, but I knew what telling you would do to you." She paused. "Codie was the reason you kept messing up in that first game, wasn't she? You weren't just rusty."

I laughed. "I'm surprised you didn't notice how hard she was flirting with me. I thought she was just playing me at first, like she could tell I was down bad for her and was just using my attraction to put me off my game, but when I overheard one of her teammates talking about her crush on me when they came to our next game, I realised it wasn't unrequited."

"And that's why you wore that miniskirt, right? At the time I thought you were still into Aaron, but you were doing it for her. I didn't even put two and two together when she started messing up."

"I'm sorry that I wasn't honest with you. But you didn't make it easy. What would you have done if I'd told you I fancied her?" I asked.

She shrugged. "Probably done all I could to put you off. I might even have warned her off you." Her eyes flicked to the right, and she smiled. "She's watching you. Well, she's talking to Ayana, but her eyes keep flitting over to you. I can tell how much you guys like each other. It's gonna take me some time to get used to seeing you together, but I'm glad that she makes you happy." She beckoned Codie over.

"I know what you think of me," Codie said to Laura, when she'd come over, "and I get it. Some of it, at least. But I love Becky, and you have my word that I'm going to treat her well."

"Look, you and I are never going to completely see eye to eye, and you'll always be my enemy on the lanes, but my best friend is head over heels for you, so what do you say we call a truce, at least outside of bowling?" Laura held her hand out.

My heart thudded in my chest as Codie stared at her for a few seconds, her expression ice queen cold—then she broke into a smile. "Deal." She took Laura's hand and gave it a shake.

From the Author

Unlike my main characters, I am not a champion bowler. However, I do enjoy a game from time to time and had always wondered what was actually involved in bowling leagues. When I thought about writing a story for this anthology, the theme of girls who meet at a bowling league sprung immediately into my mind. The research into bowling leagues was an interesting endeavour, and I hope I haven't made any major faux pas.

Obviously, conflict is at the heart of most stories, and I knew I wanted my characters to have obstacles in the way of them getting together immediately. I thought having the best friend hate the love interest would be a novel twist on the enemies to lovers trope.

I hope you enjoy spending time with Becky and Codie as much as I enjoyed writing them. I have to admit to falling slightly in love with Codie myself during the writing process. Who doesn't love a hot bitch actually hiding a heart and a personality beneath her ice queen exterior? (Just me?!)

About the Author

Katie Kent is a writer of fiction and non-fiction living in the UK with her wife, cat, and dog. She likes to write stories, mostly for a YA audience, particularly about LGTBQ characters, mental illness, time travel and the future—sometimes all in the same story! Her stories have been published in *Youth Imagination*, *Limeoncello*, *Breath and Shadow* and *Northern Gravy*, amongst others, and in a handful of anthologies including *The Trouble with Time Travel*, *Summer of Speculation: Catastrophe*, *Growth* and *My Heart to Yours*.

She won second place in *Writing Magazine*'s 2022 'Love Story' and 2023 'Age' competitions. Her non-fiction, mostly mental health-related, can be found in publications including *The Mighty*, *You & Me Magazine*, *Ailment*, *OC87 Recovery Diaries* and *Feels Zine*.

You can follow her on Twitter @uniKH80 and visit her website at https://www.katiekentwriter.com/

Always a Destroyer

by
Steven D. Brewer

Always a Destroyer

A sudden blast of wind caught me by surprise as the gust front moved across the water. At the mercy of the wind, I was blown off course—not that I had a destination in mind. I had finally given up and was merely flying farther and farther out to sea so that, when my strength was spent, I would perish without recourse. But confronted with the sudden storm, I struggled to stay aloft as a curtain of rain swept across me and drenched my wings. The temperature dropped precipitously, and I shivered in the cold rain.

A burst of hail hammered me. I tried to shield my head, but I was pounded everywhere with hammer blows of ice. The hail began to bend and break my feathers.

"How ironic," I thought bitterly. *"The valiant destroyer: after a hundred dangerous missions, she's killed by a storm."*

Between blinding sheets of rain, I spotted a tiny, rocky island below and spiraled down to a beach, where I huddled against the base of a palm tree.

Hail punched through the palm fronds, scattering fragments of leaves. Bits of vegetation clung to me as the wind rose to a crescendo. Waves blew in from the sea, drenching me with a salty spray. Somewhere behind the clouds, the sun went down. I shivered, bruised and beaten, in the dark.

The storm finally broke in the early morning hours. Dripping, cold, and miserable, I grabbed a few restless moments of sleep, shivering until the sky began to lighten.

As the sun rose, I spread my wings, tattered and broken, to let the sun begin to dry them. The sky was clear, but I was still drenched and cold, stranded on a tiny island far out in the ocean.

I looked up and down the beach for any signs of inhabitants. Sea-level rise had drowned many of the coastal buildings. The waves now lapped their broken foundations. Inland, there were a few abandoned ruins, overgrown by vegetation, with smashed windows and collapsed roofs. Looking one way down the shore, I could see nothing but empty beach. But the other way, I could see a splash of color in the distance.

A flag? A tent? I stretched my wings and flapped them a time or two but, after confirming they would not lift me, I simply started walking that way.

The ocean, which had raged during the storm, was now nearly calm. I walked at the edge of the water, where the sand was wet and firm. Small waves washed over my toes. Tiny rainbow-colored clams were revealed with each wave and then—just as quickly—buried themselves again. Frigate birds wheeled overhead. A line of pelicans flew along the shore to my right as I walked along. I mourned my battered wings that left me grounded.

As the sun climbed, I began to feel thirsty. I shaded my eyes and looked ahead. I could see now that the splash of color was a canopy set up on the beach. I was more than halfway there. Licking my lips, I pressed on.

Inland, the sand rose to an impenetrable wall of vegetation, mostly short trees with smooth, gray trunks and round leaves. Occasionally there were larger trees and, now and then, a palm. The heat might have been oppressive but for the cool sea breeze that blew inland.

I arrived at the tent. It was unoccupied. But it must have been freshly erected as it otherwise could not have survived the storm. Underneath, there was a towel laid on the sand. I looked around. Then I saw someone floating in the ocean. She had long, dark hair and pale skin. And just a hint of silvery scales. I sat in the shade of the canopy, but not on her towel, and waited.

After several minutes, she emerged from the sea, naked—as I was—and walked toward the tent. She was tall and statuesque. She spotted me as she approached and stopped.

"Who are you?" she said, her guard up.

"Just a traveler, blown off course," I replied.

"You're a destroyer," she said.

"No longer. That time is through."

She inspected me skeptically. I thought I must look terrible: dirty, gaunt, emaciated, with my wings in tatters. Filled with shame, I choked back tears and made to turn away.

"You must be thirsty," she said. "And hungry. Come. Let us share a meal."

"Thank you," I said, profoundly grateful for her hospitality, however grudging.

She picked up her towel and led me inland along a narrow path through the vegetation. The path wound some little distance back into a narrow rocky canyon. At the head of the canyon, there was a small waterfall, and, at one side, a tiny cottage nestled against a cliff.

It was constructed of pieces of coral and stone that had been cemented together. The roof had poles of timber covered with galvanized metal sheets. It was homey, in a crude and rustic way.

She bade me rinse my feet off in a small tub of water outside the door and then welcomed me inside. She poured me a cup of cool water from a pitcher, then indicated a door that led out to the waterfall.

"Why don't you take a quick shower?" she said. "You need to get the salt off. I will fix something for us to share."

I carried the cup as I drank. The water had an odd, stale, distinctive taste, but it was not unpalatable. And as parched as I was, it was glorious beyond measure.

The door she indicated opened out to a smooth, well-worn path of sandstone to where the water tumbled from overhead into the little canyon. I reached a hand out. It was cool, but not painfully cold. I ducked under the water and let it run over my head, through my hair and wings, and down my back. I turned under the stream, feeling the water run over my chest and breasts. My skin became gooseflesh and my nipples stiffened in the cool water. I shook out my wings, then ran my hands down my belly, and legs, rinsing off the salt.

When I could stand it no longer, I emerged from the waterfall, chilled and shivering. I walked back along the narrow path. She was waiting for me at the door with a fresh towel.

"Give me but a moment and I will join you on the patio," she said as she darted along the path and took her turn in the waterfall.

I shook out my wings and then, rubbing my arms and back briskly with the rough towel, I walked back through the cottage. There were only two rooms: a living area that included a kitchen and a small, private bedroom. I walked through the kitchen and found a doorway out to the patio.

As I reached the door, I heard her voice from the waterfall as she began to sing. She had an enchanting voice that rose and fell in no language I could discern. It was hauntingly beautiful and brought tears to my eyes.

I stepped outside. On a wide shelf of sandstone, beside the stream that flowed down from the waterfall, the patio was bounded by a wall of rock that dripped with lichens, mosses, and ferns. There was a small, red clay chiminea next to a table with two chairs.

I selected the seat farther from the house, where I could look back to watch for her approach. A small fire had been laid in the chiminea that produced a surprising amount of warmth, which I found welcome in the cool, rocky defile. And it filled the atmosphere with a lovely scent of piney smoke.

The table was laid with small plates and a platter that had a napkin covering its contents. I was left to guess what delights might await me. I began to salivate with hunger and anticipation. But I leaned back in the chair to patiently await my host.

In just moments, she emerged from the house carrying a large carafe and two cups.

"Coffee?" she asked.

"Please."

After she poured it out, she removed the napkin from the plate, revealing a small mound of scones.

My stomach growled, which made her smile.

"Please help yourself," she said.

I selected two of the larger scones, and she offered me honey to drizzle over them. I waited to sample them until she had served herself.

We ate in silence for several moments. They were delicious and, with the coffee, went a long way toward restoring my spirits. After eating the first two scones, I looked up and she gestured that I should take more. I took three more, smothered them with honey and, reminding myself to savor them fully, ate them with great relish. I licked my long fingers and recurved claws carefully.

"What brings a destroyer here?" she said.

"Please," I said. "I am not a destroyer any longer."

"Once a destroyer, always a destroyer," she said harshly. "I have seen what your kind will do."

I noticed her word choice. Not "can do," but "will do."

I stood and bowed. "I am only here by chance. I have no mission here. I will leave as soon as I am able."

"You have no mission here…" she said. "Then where?"

"I have no mission anywhere," I admitted. "There are no more missions."

She pursed her lips. "How long before you can leave?"

"My feathers will regrow within a week," I said. "With adequate nutrition."

"Very well," she said. "You will stay here. Where I can keep an eye on you."

"By your leave. And what should I call you?"

"Melody," she said. "And you are?"

"Last," I said.

She raised her eyebrows.

"When we were created, we were given only numbers. But I was the last. And I believe I *am* the last. We were not built to last. Yet here I am."

"Here you are," she said. "We—none of us—have been treated kindly by fate."

"You seem to be well enough," I said.

She eyed me, then sighed.

"Yes. Compared with many, I am well enough. But I was made to serve people. And there are no longer any people to serve."

"Are there no people on the island?"

She shook her head. "I don't believe so. I haven't seen any for more than a year. I used to see boats offshore, but I haven't for a long while. Perhaps there are no longer any people anywhere."

"No. There still are," I said. "On the mainland. There are still arcologies. But after the biowars, they can no longer come out without…"

"Without getting sick from the persistent spores."

After several moments of silence, I asked, "So what can I do to earn my keep?"

"Can you do the laundry?"

"If you tell me what to do…"

She gave me directions and I carried a large basket of clothes and bedding down a narrow path to the stream and spent an hour pounding the laundry on rocks. I had to be careful not to snag the fabric with my claws. Next, I carried everything out to the beach where she had a clothesline in the sun. Finally, after everything was hung up, I laid down and napped in the tent, grateful to finally be warm enough.

As sunset approached, she came out and invited me to swim in the ocean with her.

"I will help you bring in the laundry," she said. "And then I have dinner ready."

Floating in the water, we looked west toward the setting sun.

"It's like paradise," she said.

"A paradise. Without people."

"I guess that's what paradise is."

After bringing in the laundry and rinsing off under the waterfall, I returned to the patio. There were two large pans on the table. Stomach growling, I took my seat and awaited Melody.

When she arrived, she brought a taper from the stove and lit three torches that surrounded the table. They cast a red and flickering light in the darkness. In the tropics, the sun went straight down, and just a few minutes after sunset, it was already fully dark.

"I hope you like it," she said, lifting the covers on the pots.

"It smells delicious," I said, mouth watering. I served myself a generous helping of rice then dipped the spoon into the other pot. "What is this?" I asked.

"It's conch," she said. "I'm afraid I'm limited in what ingredients I can get, so my repertoire is somewhat limited. I fear you will find it tedious before long."

"Um…" I said, my mouth full. "I doubt it. I'm just grateful to have anything to eat."

After dinner, I helped her clear the table and wash the dishes. Then she handed me a pillow and a blanket.

"You may sleep on the couch. Goodnight."

"Thank you," I said, feeling genuinely grateful.

She retired to her bedroom and shut the door.

I laid down on the couch and shifted around, pulling the blanket around me. I closed my eyes. Sleep eluded me, however.

I kept remembering the camaraderie of my fellow destroyers. We had always been treated as elites. We had received the best of everything and slept communally, happily pressed together. To be reduced to feeling gratitude for the charity of a stranger overwhelmed me. I had fallen so far. And I was so lonely! I couldn't help myself and started to cry. I turned over and forced my face into the pillow, trying to smother my sobs.

I heard Melody open her bedroom door.

"Are you lonely too?" she asked.

I tried to answer but couldn't make any words come out. I just nodded, sobbing incoherently.

"Come," she said. She reached out a hand. I stood, stepped forward, took her hand, and let her draw me into her bedroom. She pulled her covers back and laid down with her back to me. I cuddled up against her back, pressed my face between her shoulder blades, and breathed in her scent. The skin on her back was warm and covered with soft scales.

"Thank you," I mumbled, overwhelmed with gratitude. "Thank you. Thank you!" And, in moments, I felt sleep take me.

I awoke alone in the bed. Rain was hammering on the metal roof and gurgling in the downspouts. I yawned and stretched. Then got up and walked out to the kitchen where Melody was pulling a pan out of the oven.

"More scones?" I asked. She nodded. I looked out on the patio, where it was pouring rain. We stood together in the kitchen and ate the scones.

"Where do you get your food?"

"In the early days of the war, after all the people were dead— or gone—there was still food in grocery stores. But then I found a warehouse with several shipping containers of merchandise. Flour. Rice. Beans. Oil. There is enough to last for years."

"But nothing perishable."

"No. No milk. Or butter. Or meat—I am not a hunter. Fish, I can get. And conch."

We ate in silence for several minutes, then I said, "Thank you."

"For the food?"

"Well, yes. But… But I was thinking of last night."

"I never would have imagined a destroyer feeling lonely," she said.

"We were created to work together. As a team. Being alone, with no mission, is… It's like… Life has no meaning."

"Where were you flying to, way out here?" she asked.

I looked down and didn't answer.

"You… You weren't flying anywhere, were you?"

"No. I was just going to fly until I couldn't fly anymore," I muttered. "But in the end, I couldn't even do that."

"Oh, Last!" she said. She suddenly reached forward and carefully took my hands, mindful of the claws. "I'm glad you couldn't."

I couldn't meet her eyes and began to snuffle with self-pity.

After breakfast, with the rain continuing to fall, she led me back to her bedroom and pulled me under the covers with her again. This time, I buried my head in her chest as I shook with sobs. I struggled to rein in my emotions. Her hand touched my arm, then my wing. I felt her fingers run through my feathers, which calmed me like nothing else. Her warmth and softness gradually lulled me back to sleep.

It was afternoon when I awoke again. The house was silent and empty, so, after a few minutes, I walked down the path toward the ocean. As I approached, I could see a boat anchored just offshore. Then I heard her scream.

I sprinted. When the canopy came into view, I could see that two men were holding her down in the tent while a third tried to force himself on her. My rage became incandescent and then, just as suddenly, I was a destroyer once more. Calm settled over me as I accepted the mission before me.

"What's that?" one said, catching sight of me approaching.

"It's a destroyer! Kill it!"

He grabbed a large-bore rifle that had been by his side. The biological projector in my chest lit up and the beam weapon, for which destroyers were known, vaporized the upper part of his body. Truncated, his torso flopped down, spilling the steaming contents of his abdominal cavity. The others tried to flee but, walking forward, I destroyed them as they ran, leaving only smoking, charred remains in the sand.

"They are dead," I said, when I reached the canopy. I looked down at Melody. Her face was puffy and swollen. I could see bruises where they had beaten her. And there were marks around her wrists where they had held her.

Like a sudden shower of cold water, I realized that I was afraid to meet her eyes or touch her. I turned to go.

"Where are you going?" she asked.

"Once a destroyer, always a destroyer," I said. "You told me so yourself."

"I'm...I'm glad you're a destroyer," she said.

I paused, then turned back and extended my hand.

From the Author

This weird little story weaves together a bunch of imagery that has played out in my imagination for many years.

The setting is an island, strongly influenced by my many visits to a Caribbean island. The time is vaguely in the future, after an apocalyptic war that has left the remaining humanity sheltering in arcologies due to persistent bioweapon spores.

And the characters are artificially constructed organisms: one is the embodiment of an elite weapon that used to be treated with great respect and privilege. She is now viewed, not unreasonably perhaps, with distrust and suspicion. The other was constructed to serve people—but now all of the people she used to serve are gone.

Thrown together by circumstance, these two very different characters must try to understand each other—and themselves.

About the Author

Steven D. Brewer teaches scientific writing at the University of Massachusetts Amherst. As an author, Brewer identifies diverse obsessions that underlie his writing: deep interests in natural history, life science, and environmentalism; an abiding passion for languages; a fascination with Japanese culture; and a mania for information technology and the Internet. Brewer lives in Amherst, Massachusetts with his extended family.

Barley

by
Evan Purcell

Barley

It was a normal Saturday night in my post-relationship life, which meant that I was alone in the nearest convenience store buying a microwavable dinner for one.

That was what my life had turned into. I slid my change across the counter and the small, blandly polite cashier gave me my pitiful box of dinner.

"Thanks," I mumbled. Normally, I'd engage in a bit of small talk with the guy, but tonight I didn't bother.

Instead, he initiated the conversation. Speaking with an accent I couldn't identify, he said, "I wonder what's bugging him."

"Who?" I asked. There was no one else in the store.

The man, probably about fifty and with a world-weariness around his eyes that made him look about sixty, nodded his head toward the door.

I turned.

The entire front wall was glass, which gave me a good view of the street outside. There, walking alone, was a man who looked about my age. He seemed a bit hunched over, and he was wiping his face.

"What do you mean?" I asked. The guy seemed normal, if a bit in a hurry.

"Look closer," the guy told me. "His shirt is half-untucked. He's crying."

I did look closer, just as the stranger paused to wipe his face, and when I did, his sadness struck me like a hammer. How had I not noticed that before?

"I don't know," I told the cashier. "Never seen the guy before."

I grabbed my change—a whole eight cents—and sprinkled each coin into the little give-a-penny take-a-penny tray. Then I hurried outside.

Why was I hurrying? Did I really want to talk to some wounded stranger? Did I really need human interaction so badly that I literally power-walked out the door?

Yeah. I kind of did.

"Hey!" I shouted. "Wait."

The man didn't turn around. If anything, he quickened his pace.

"Excuse me?" I tried again.

His answer was more of an inaudible mumble than actual words. He still didn't look at me.

"Do you need help?" I tried again. I kept my voice softer than usual. I didn't want to scare him off.

He stopped and turned. Finally. I got a good look at his face, and at the red rings around his dark eyes. "Do I look like I need help?" he asked.

"Actually, yeah." I walked toward him, and he half-recoiled, as if I was about to tackle him to the ground like a linebacker. It wasn't the first time I'd gotten that reaction out of someone.

"Do I know you?" he asked. For such a slight man—of average height but noticeably thin—he had a deep voice. Soft, if a little impatient, but deep, too.

"Uh…" I started.

His face was red and puffy but also handsome. He had dark eyes, almost black, and an angular face that terminated into a neat goatee. He looked like the dictionary definition of a tortured artist.

And I had seen him before. I knew him.

"Um, yeah?" I said. "I think so." I studied him. How did I know those dark eyes? "I think we live in the same building," I added, to both him and myself.

He half-smiled, which was a definite improvement from the non-smile that he had maintained up until that point. "Yeah," he admitted. "You're below me."

"Well, if you're walking home," I said, "and I'm walking home, why don't we walk home together?"

"What's this about?" he asked.

"What do you mean?"

He crossed his arms. "I mean," he spelled out, "if this is because you're pitying me or something…"

"No," I protested. I was in no place to judge anybody else, not at this point in my life. "Of course not. It's practical. We're going in the same direction."

Quick save.

And I think he bought it. His frown softened into something...well, not exactly happy, but at least neutral. He started walking and I kept stride.

"Trent," I said by way of introduction.

"Barley," he responded.

"Barley. Like the..."

"Beer ingredient," he cut me off. Apparently, he'd heard that before. A lot. "Yeah. My parents were free thinkers. I have a little brother named Coda."

"Wow." I didn't know what to say.

"Trent is normal."

Was that a compliment?

"My *name* is, anyway," I admitted. "Me, not so much." I worked in construction. I was a foreman. I did pretty well for myself, despite not having a college education, and I might have seemed normal on paper. But I knew, from the depth of my own self-awareness, that I was anything but.

Barley got this far-off look, like he was imagining a different life for himself. "Normal names are the best," he said. "When I have kids, I'm going all in. Tom and Jane. Maybe something with an M, like Mark or Michael or Mary. Life is hard enough as is."

"Tell me about it," I muttered.

He froze. Stopped dead in his tracks. "Don't humor me, okay?"

I stopped, too. "What?" I asked.

Did I say something wrong? I thought our conversation was going well.

"Clearly, I'm in a not-great place right now," he said. "I wish I could hide it, but I can't. This is a low point. Obviously. And it might seem nice to sympathize or whatever, but I really don't want to talk about it."

I didn't know what "it" was. But whatever he meant by the pronoun, I could tell that he didn't want me to press him too hard. "Okay," I conceded.

"And I don't want to hear about your problems, either," he added. Then he looked down, his eyes falling on the TV dinner that I carried against my chest. It must've been a pretty pathetic sight, because his tone instantly softened. "Sorry. I'm being kinda rude, huh?"

"Little bit," I admitted.

"Come on."

He started walking again. It took me a few steps to catch up. He moved quickly, purposefully, but I kept pace. Together, we crossed the street. In a minute, we'd reached our building.

I waited for him to enter first. He did the same. We were both being gentlemanly, I guess. Eventually, he went first and I followed. He held the door open behind him. His movements were smooth, almost too smooth. He was gay, I could tell, but I wasn't sure if he could tell that I was. I never had the same kind of sway to my movements that guys like Barley had. I guess that made my life easier. I could blend in a bit more. At the same time, though, I found someone like Barley, someone with that almost-seductive sense of motion, extremely sexy.

We both crossed to the elevator. No one was in the lobby, as usual. Sometimes we had a doorman, but he was typically AWOL. Tonight, I was a bit grateful to be alone with Barley, even just for a few minutes. It was better than making the walk home by myself.

The elevator doors closed in front of us and we stood together in silence. I pressed the third button and he pressed the fourth. Trying to fill the silence, I said, "Tomorrow will be better."

Why did I say that? Did I really believe it? Did I have enough information about this total stranger to really make that sort of prediction?

He shrugged. "Nowhere to go but up."

"Is that an elevator pun?" I asked, mostly as a way to lighten a bit of the darkness that had edged into the conversation.

For the first time since I saw him, he chuckled. It was a nice chuckle, something rare and genuine. He covered his mouth, as if the chuckle had somehow revealed some dark secret about himself, something that he wanted to hide.

Ding.

We reached the third floor, which was my cue to get off. I didn't want to leave. Not yet. But I couldn't just stand there and smile back at him. That would've been really awkward. I edged toward the open door.

"Thanks," he muttered, as if the word was hard for him to say.

I stopped. I waited for him to elaborate.

"For, you know, walking with me," he said. It could've been sarcasm on his part, but I really didn't think so. It seemed like he was genuinely thanking me.

I didn't expect that.

"Any time," I told him. "Just being neighborly."

In our last moment together, I had the unmistakable urge to kiss him, to grab him by the shoulders and connect with him physically, in a way that would claim him as mine forever. But this was life, not some cheesy romance novel, so I didn't. I left. As the elevator doors closed between us, he said one more thing: "Enjoy your TV dinner."

And the doors shut. He was gone.

Standing in my hallway, alone, with my box dinner held tightly to my chest, I realized that I'd probably never find out what his problem was.

Maybe that was for the best.

An hour later, I found myself staring at my microwave and thinking about Barley. As the little tray of food spun in circles, and as my eyes followed its repetitive little path, I thought about the charming curve of his mouth. I thought about the way he walked, the fluidity that made his movements seem like some sort of dance.

Barley.

I barely talked to the guy. Why did I keep thinking about him?

Still, it was better than thinking about my ex, which is what I had been doing pretty non-stop for the last few months.

I needed some fresh air. At the very least, I needed to get out of this tiny, empty apartment before I bashed my head against that stupid, whirring microwave.

I turned it off—the microwave—and headed toward the elevator. In times like these, I went up to the rooftop. It didn't have the best view of the city, but it was good enough. And the night breeze would at least keep me company for a few minutes.

Five floors later, I had made it onto the roof. The night had gotten colder in the hour I'd been inside, but the cold air would do me good. Help me keep my mind off of things.

I froze. There, up ahead, was a man standing on the edge of the roof. He was dangerously close to falling off.

I needed to warn him.

Him. Barley? Yeah. It had to be Barley. He was facing the other direction, but I recognized his slim build, not to mention the childlike way he wrapped his arms around himself.

"Barley?" I asked.

The figure turned, and I knew that he most definitely was the memorably named resident of the fourth floor. He recognized me just as soon as I recognized him. He swore loudly.

"Barley, please," I said. "Get down from there. It's not safe."

That was when I realized that he must've been there for a reason. No one stands on the edge of a roof unless they have the urge to jump.

I approached him slowly, held out my hand like an animal trainer walking toward a lion. "Whatever happened to you today," I said, "this isn't the answer."

He stepped off the ledge and onto the concrete roof. "Christ, Trent, I came up here to think," he said. "I wasn't going to…you know."

"Good," I whispered. I didn't quite believe him, though. "Still. Can you back away from the ledge a little more? You know, just in case."

He gave me a look that could wither paint. He hated me, at least according to that look. But he started approaching me. That was what really mattered, after all. He wasn't in the danger zone anymore. He stopped just a few feet from me. We both stood in the center of the roof. Safe.

His arms were crossed. He didn't have anything to say to me.

I figured I'd have to fill the silence. "So," I said. "What did you come up here to think about?"

"I don't know," he answered. "Lots of things."

I raised my eyebrow. I still couldn't tell if he was being honest with me. With guys like this—so haunted, so closed off—it was always hard to tell.

He added, "Mostly related to how I'm recently single."

I laughed. Now things were clicking into place. "I see."

"No, you don't," Barley insisted. "Because I'm not some heart-broken guy. I'm happy to be single again. It's great."

I stepped closer to him. I felt actual, physical heat in the air between us. The rest of the night air was cold, but that little space between us was warming fast. "Somehow, I don't believe you," I told him.

"It is," he insisted. "Shut up. I'm just..." He breathed, and it sounded like a piece of him, a broken part, disappeared from his breath and into the night air. "Me and Hudson, my ex, we had plenty of problems the last few months. And I was planning to break up with him. But he beat me to it. And I'm kind of pissed off about it, actually."

He was revealing so much about himself. I didn't know what to say. "Is that why you were crying earlier?" I finally asked.

"Jesus!" he shouted. "What is your problem?"

The outburst came out of nowhere. Well, maybe I was pushing him a bit too hard. "Nothing. I—"

"No," he shouted, "it's something. I hate when you straight guys look at us like we're these over-sensitive, delicate types."

I didn't correct him. Instead, I said, "You, uh, seem to hate a lot of things."

Somehow, that got to him. He allowed his face to soften. His red-lined eyes, previously narrowed into slits, seemed to widen, to finally look at me for the first time since I stepped onto this roof.

"Maybe that's my character flaw," he admitted.

I looked at him quizzically. What was he getting at? He sounded like a psychiatrist or something.

Apparently, I'd made a look, because he answered my unspoken question: "I'm a playwright," he said. "I like to look at people and boil all their problems down to one, overarching character flaw."

"Yeah?"

He looked away. "Maybe mine is that I'm too sensitive."

"Or that you're too angry over being too sensitive," I countered.

He smiled. His face lit up. It was one of the most sudden, wonderful smiles I'd ever seen. "Trent," he said. "That was slightly insightful."

My heart quickened at his sudden enthusiasm, but I forced myself to ignore it. "And what's mine?" I asked him.

At first, he didn't understand. Then he did: "Your character flaw?"

"Yeah."

He cocked an eyebrow, looked me up and down. He scanned me like a doctor looking at an X-ray. "I don't know yet," he answered. "Maybe the incessant need to help others, even when they clearly don't want the help."

Touché.

He was right, of course. I was the kind of guy who spent a lot of time swooping in and rescuing people, whether they needed it or not. In another life, I was probably a firefighter or a monk or something.

But that wasn't my overarching flaw. Not by a long shot. If someone asked me what my big, bad character flaw was, I'd only have one answer: loneliness. Or more specifically, the constant need to make a connection.

I didn't say that, though. I couldn't.

"You have a family?" he asked. "Wife? Kids?"

Hardly.

I shook my head. No family, chosen or otherwise. My biological family was back in Nebraska and my would-be family, my former fiancé, was gone for good. Last December, Michael left me. Broke off our engagement. He was married to a woman now, and I was still reeling, despite the months that had already passed.

"I, um, I had a fiancé," I answered. "Didn't work out."

"I see," he said. An expression flashed across his dark eyes, something I couldn't quite read. It was like he was asking himself whether he wanted to continue our conversation. He eventually added, "Well, I just had a boyfriend. But we were pretty serious. Talking about kids and stuff."

"But I thought you said the relationship had gone bad," I said.

"Yeah. Recently." He sniffled. It was turning into a cold night. "But for the longest time, things were good."

"What changed?" I asked.

For me, the big change was when my fiancé decided that he wanted to be straight again. *Big* change. It was a single conversation, both of us standing in the middle of our kitchen, when Michael declared that our "lifestyle" wasn't working for him. We were happy. We were normal. And then, well, Michael's life has apparently gotten a lot more "normal" since then. Mine had only gotten lonelier.

Whatever. Screw 'im.

I should've known, though. I really should've. Things had been feeling off for a few months before that kitchen conversation. Michael had been pulling away in slow motion, and I just didn't allow myself to notice. I should've.

"What changed?" Barley parroted my words. "I did, I guess. I was always a struggling writer, and I think Hudson liked that. He liked being the provider or whatever. But last year, I started workshopping a new play, *Hazy Blue*, and it has sort of blown up."

"Blown up" was an understatement. I didn't really follow live theater, but even I knew that *Hazy Blue* was this year's big phenomenon. There was literally a poster of it near the convenience store. It was one of those small-cast dramas about a family in the midst of imploding. Pretty standard live theater stuff. And yet, there was something special in its specific alchemy. People seemed to love it.

Barley, I guess, was a pretty talented guy.

"And I'm not..." he continued. "Well, I'm not struggling anymore. I thought that would be a good thing. But it seems like Hudson didn't."

"He was jealous?" I asked.

Barley shrugged. "Apparently," he admitted. "I don't know. Mostly insecure." He turned away, effectively cutting himself off from our conversation.

"Okay," I said.

He would've kept staring into the distance, but something drew him back toward me. He scanned me up and down. Did he like what he saw? I couldn't tell.

"I still don't get why you were so upset," I told him. "I mean, break-ups are tough, but...you came up here."

"I'm not suicidal," he answered, as if that cleared everything up.

"I didn't say that," I said quickly. I implied it, and I most certainly thought it, but I didn't say anything.

"I'm not," he kept going. "I'm sad. And that's normal."

"Yeah. Totally."

It was a full moon tonight, and even though everything was dimmed by the unblinking lights of the city below, the moon was still aggressively bright. Too bright.

We stood there in silence. Together. The warmth between us intensified.

"Look," he said. "Thanks for your neighborly concern or whatever, but I'm good. I don't need some dashing, straight individual to swoop in and save me. I'm at a low point, and that's natural. Low points are necessary for our character development."

"You sure talk like a writer," I said.

He winced at the comment.

"But," I added, "you're a bit mistaken about me."

"Yeah?" he pressed. "You're not dashing?"

"No. I am. Clearly." It was meant as a joke.

"Oh," he said, dragging out the syllable into a full-on sentence. "You're not straight."

I shook my head. Not at all. Not since I was old enough to understand what sexual attraction even was. Not since I opened up a Batman comic and started looking at the Caped Crusader in a whole new light.

"You're lucky," Barley said.

Not the typical response to a coming out.

"Because I'm gay?" I asked.

"Because you can pass," he answered. He looked at his feet, not at me. "You can keep secrets secret and no one would suspect anything. Me, not so much." As if to prove a point, he gestured wildly.

"So you're one of those self-hating gays that I see on TV," I said, my words pushing him further than he wanted to go.

"Shut up," he said.

"No. It's fine," I told him, not letting up. "The world needs all kinds. I guess most writers are self-hating. Explains the rooftop."

"For the last time," he shouted, "I wasn't gonna jump!" His eyes flashed genuine anger, but they cooled just as quickly.

"So, when was your break-up?" I asked.

"Huh?" he responded. He rubbed his goatee with his thumb and forefinger. It seemed like a nervous habit, though I hadn't noticed him do that before.

"With that Hudson guy," I said. I'd never met this Hudson before, but I had a picture of him in my head. Handsome. Blonde. Aww-shucks Midwestern. I wasn't sure why I had that image. "When did it happen?"

"A few weeks ago," he admitted.

"So, what made you cry tonight?" I asked. "What brought you up here?"

He looked at me, finally lowering whatever shield he'd kept suspended around him. "My family," he said. His eyes never left mine. There was pain in them, but he didn't bother hiding that pain from me.

"Your..." I started.

"Family. Yes."

"They don't approve," I guessed.

I could relate. Certainly. Before I came out to my parents, they never expected there was anything different with me. They treated me just like my brothers. Then, after the conversation to end all conversations, things turned very, very different. I hadn't seen my parents in over a year.

I even went down to visit them once, back when Michael and I were in the midst of our honeymoon phase, and they had said they were too sick to have guests. "The flu," they said. "Contagious," they said. "Intolerance," they implied.

"No," he explained. "They... Well, they didn't for the longest time. I'm from Georgia. Anyway, they sort of wrote me off, my mom especially. But then they met Hudson, and he charmed them immediately. He could do that, the bastard. And he talked about our future plans and stuff. And my mom—in the midst of that *gimme-grandkids* fever that all moms get—she sort of came around. They all did. Because of Hudson."

"And then the break-up happened," I ventured.

"And then the break-up happened," he repeated. "I haven't told them about it yet. Kept putting it off. But then Mom called and said that she was coming up here for a visit. Wanted to see my show. She was finally putting the effort in. And I couldn't say no."

"So did you tell them?" I asked.

He shook his head, his long-ish hair wagging messily around his face. "No," he said. "It would change things, you know?"

I didn't know. *He* didn't know, either.

"Maybe not," I said. "I mean, once a family member comes around, they come around. At least, that's my experience."

I wasn't speaking from *actual* experience, of course. My own family hadn't come around yet. They didn't even show up to my big engagement party. And their over-the-phone coldness hadn't changed when I got together with Michael, nor had it changed when the two of us broke up. Instead, my family had spent most of my adult life giving me steady waves of grudging tolerance, which wasn't ideal, obviously.

Still, I knew that once they did come around, they wouldn't change their mind and start rejecting me again.

At least, I hoped that wouldn't happen.

"Wish it were that easy," he said.

"What if it were?" I asked. "What if it really were that easy?"

He didn't answer.

I continued, "Sounds to me like you're imagining the worst, and the worst hasn't even happened yet."

He shrugged.

"Does that mean you agree with me?" I asked.

"Maybe," he admitted. He approached me, his footsteps echoing loudly. Aside from those footsteps, the night was pretty quiet up there. All the street sounds below were muffled by distance.

And the closer he got, the more I could feel the magnetic pull that he had over me. And the heat. The warmth had slowly turned into heat, and that heat wasn't going away any time soon. My feet stayed in one place, but I could feel myself leaning forward.

"You, uh, you're pretty smart," he said. "Insightful."

"Sure," I answered, my reflexes telling me to brush away the compliment. "Smart" wasn't an adjective I heard a lot.

Ever, really. I think I was too big, too lumbering, for people to see me and think that I was smart. I was blue-collar smart, street-smart. But people didn't usually notice that kind of intelligence in a person.

"Thanks," he added.

"For what?"

He placed his hands on my waist. "For swooping in. I mean…"

"No problem," I told him. I laughed a little, just to fill the silence.

And he kissed me.

It was a sudden, unexpected, inevitable kiss. I knew I wanted him, but I didn't realize I wanted him that badly until his lips were on mine, his hands were on my sides, and his gentle breathing matched tempos with my own.

I hadn't kissed someone like this since...well, ever. Michael and I had some good make-out sessions in the past, but it never felt this natural. I almost couldn't believe how well his body fit against mine.

His fingers thrummed a secret melody along the side of my torso. He was playing me, like some piano. His head tilted. Mine did, too. And his warm tongue slid over mine. He guided my body, not the other way around, and I liked that. I liked giving in.

He pulled away first.

"That was...unexpected," I muttered, out of breath.

"Why?" he asked, his tone of voice implying that I was somehow the biggest stud in the world.

"I don't know," I answered. My voice cracked. "It's just been a while. Don't let my dashing exterior fool you. I'm a bit more damaged than I come across."

He kissed me again, this time a quick peck on my upper lip. "Perfect," he said. "That's my type."

I breathed slowly. I needed to ask him something, but I didn't know how to say it. Finally, even though I fumbled a little with my words, I asked, "Can you be honest with me? Just for a second?"

"I've *been* honest," he said, his voice a mixture of intrigued and frustrated.

"No," I said. "I mean, I'm going to ask you a question, and I'd like you to promise me that you'll give me a real, honest answer."

He studied me for the longest time. He didn't blink. He didn't move. Finally, he replied, "Okay."

Good.

And my question: "Were you thinking about jumping? When you came up here?"

He flinched at my question. Perhaps I did, too.

For a moment, I was sure that he wasn't going to answer me.

Then he said, "Honestly? I don't even know." It felt like a real answer. An honest one. He added, "But I *can* tell you, again, with all honesty, that I'm not thinking about it now."

"Good." It was the only response I had. Well, that and kissing him once more. He expected it this time, and allowed himself to lean in. Just a bit. I playfully bit into his full lower lip, eliciting a sharp exhale from him. Then our lips locked into place, I held him close, and his warmth spilled into me.

He was going to be okay.

I was going to be okay.

He pulled away again. "Come to my place," he said. "I'll make you dinner."

I smiled at the offer. I had no way of knowing if Barley was a good cook, but even if he wasn't, I was sure that anything he made would be an improvement over my pitiful microwave dinner for one. "Okay," I said.

He laughed.

"What's so funny?"

"In my writing," he explained, "I always push my characters into these dark places. And then I give them sudden reversals of fortune. The bad and the good, one right after the other. It's cathartic."

"So this is a good moment?" I asked.

"One of the best." He considered his words, before clarifying: "Well, it feels like the beginning of a good moment, anyway."

I didn't say anything, because we both started walking back toward the stairs, but I knew exactly what he meant. I agreed with him.

This was the beginning of, well, something. I wasn't sure what.

My brain flashed through visions of future dinners, of meeting his visiting parents, of being the boyfriend that they would want for their son. I pictured myself replacing Hudson, a man that I'd never met and barely knew anything about. And I pictured things going smoothly.

I even pictured my own family coming for a visit, somehow changing their deep-rooted problems and religious hang-ups. I pictured Barley serving my parents a platter of finger foods while I poured them wine. I pictured so many things. *Too* many things.

Who knew if any of my hopeful predictions would come to fruition? This might just be a nice dinner between neighbors. But I doubted that.

This time, things *felt* different.

I knew it. And I think Barley knew it, too.

When the future eventually arrived—if I got to be a real, lingering part of his life—I hoped I wouldn't disappoint. I hoped I was dashing enough. We would see.

But in the meantime, I knew I wasn't going to have any microwave dinners for a while.

From the Author

The idea for my story, "Barley," started at a 7-Eleven in Bangkok, Thailand. I had just gotten into the city and hadn't made any local friends yet. As I was shopping, I noticed another foreigner through the front windows. He was hurrying across the street with his head down and his hands in his pockets. I honestly don't remember what he looked like, but I remember the body language. He seemed like he needed someone to talk to. I thought about running outside and asking if he was okay, but I didn't have the nerve. I never saw him again.

For some reason, I kept thinking about that stranger. I'd seen him through a window for less than a minute, and yet I couldn't stop wondering what his story was. Did he need my help? Would I have made a difference if I had been confident enough to go outside and talk to him? It was such a short, unimportant moment in my life, but I kept inflating its significance in my head.

A month later, my visa expired, and I had to leave the country. On my last night there, I ended up running around to different shops to buy last-minute gifts for my friends. I was hurrying through a parking lot not too far from that 7-Eleven, and I realized that I was walking just like that stranger had: head down, hands in my pockets. If someone saw me, they might think that I was upset over something, but I wasn't. I was just in a hurry.

And as I finished my shopping, the whole story of "Barley" began to form in my mind. What if I had talked to that stranger? What if that one conversation would change both our lives?

That probably wouldn't have happened, but it's a fun thing to think about.

About the Author

Evan Purcell is a writer and educator who has lived everywhere from Zanzibar to Bhutan. He managed summer camps in Kazakhstan, taught drama in Ukraine, assisted volunteer dentists in Cambodia, and helped over 200 children from developing countries publish their first stories and poems.

He's written novels, plays, podcasts, and cartoons, and his very first film (a low-budget gay slasher) is ready to film later this year.

You can find more information about his latest projects on his website: www.evanpurcellromance.com.

Facebook: www.facebook.com/EvanPurcellWriter

or

Medium: medium.com/@evan_purcell

If you're curious about his new movie, you can find all the information here: www.therememberfilm.com

The *Company* We Keep

by
Natasia Langfelder

The *Company* We Keep

Ruby

Ruby felt the slimy weed wind itself through her legs. She kicked, but the harder she struggled, the more she entwined herself with the vine. She felt it pulling her to the bottom of the lake, just like her mother said it would. To the cold drowning depths. Her mother's cackle. The tickle and itch of hornwort along her body. The cold drowning depths.

She awoke with a start. There were no lakes where she was going. And she wasn't drowning...not in water at least. Her room on the space shuttle was small, and she shared it with another woman who was snoring lightly on the bunk below her. They had a small round window that let them look out into the stars. At first, the view was a novelty, but she had grown sick of them and started turning away from the window to sleep.

"Are we there yet?" she asked herself. She remembered when her children used to ask her that. They drove her crazy with that question, now she had to be content with asking herself.

Are we there yet are we there yet are we there yet? She considered taking another sleeping pill. The instructor at the institute had said it would be easier to just take the pills and sleep until arrival.

"Why make the journey harder for yourself than it needs to be?" the Company instructor had said, standing at the head of the classroom, in front of a pathetic cadre of about ten sad women in metal chairs at children's desks. Ruby's butt had ached from the chair digging into her hips. The pages of the orientation booklet hung off the sides of the cold, Formica slab. "The journey will feel like a lunar month. There are no side effects to these." The instructor shook a blue bottle and held up a large yellow capsule. Just wake up, eat, and pop another one. Oh, and don't forget to eat." She'd chuckled. "You don't want to starve to death." She had hesitated and the smile fell off her face. "Seriously, don't starve to death."

Ruby eyed the yellow pill and debated going down to the cafeteria to eat. She swallowed the pill and turned back onto her side.

Annie

Annie knew the route her new Companion was traveling would be hard and wondered where they had found the woman to do it. Staring out the window of the house, her thoughts wandered. She had requested the homestead be styled like an old-fashioned Montana ranch, not that she had ever seen one outside of a history book. The smooth stone and wooden arches, the incorporation of nature, roughhewn, helped her feel connected to something bigger than herself. She liked to imagine Earth's first pioneers would approve.

The representative from the Company had smiled when she chose it. "That's certainly original. You'll stand out when you have neighbors."

"When or if?" Annie asked, and the smile fell off that good Company representative's face. Annie tended to have that effect on people.

The homestead was mostly for mental health, to keep you sane. Encased in a polyethylene bubble, which tamed the powerful UV rays from Kepler-62 and contained the pumped-in oxygen, it gave the homestead a sense of normalcy.

God, she would love a smoke right now. Annie closed her eyes and remembered the feeling of the VapO'nic stick between her lips. But the contract she had signed with the Company prohibited smoking, or anything that would cause further damage to her lungs. It was standard really, none of the Kepler 62F pioneers could do anything that would endanger their health. Endangering your health meant endangering your station, endangering your station meant your post would be empty, and if there were empty posts, the jobs needed to keep the whole operation running would collapse.

Annie's job was important because it was a moneymaker. Annie's job was hard because it was a moneymaker. She could do it alone, but the Company was convinced that humans are social creatures and that every employee needed a Companion. The Company was optimistic that within ten Earth years' time, they would have neighbors and a community.

There were mockups of large community centers, with restaurants and shops. Someplace you could go dancing. Annie loved slow dancing. She loved the pressure points where you connected with someone: cheek, hip, hand. But that was forever away and, quite frankly, possibly a Company pipe dream. They could all blow up before any of that came to pass.

The only people she saw were maintenance employees who came to check on the homestead mechanics and the supply drop drones, who didn't have much to offer in the way of conversation.

"The Company wants to create a happy, healthy home for you and your Companion where you can both thrive," said the video representative that popped up on the tablet screen in her home office.

So you don't go insane from loneliness, Annie thought.

"We've created a questionnaire that will help us procure the perfect companion for you. Estimated time of completion, four hours."

The first two portions were all about Annie. What were her day-to-day habits? Did she prefer to keep a clean home? How would she describe her sense of humor? Did she prefer to be around others or alone? Was she a cat person or a dog person? What was her love language?

Most of the answers came easily, although after a few hours she was sick of thinking about herself. Then the questionnaire shifted to what she wanted from a potential partner.

It started with the physical, which Annie was pretty flexible on, and she flew through the answers by mostly checking "e: not very important." But when she got to the personality portion, she hesitated. She had never been good at selecting romantic partners. Her relationships always ended in disaster. Her last girlfriend had thrown a toaster at her head and honestly, she deserved it. She decided to leave the boxes blank. *Let's leave it to fate,* she thought, and clicked Submit.

Ruby

"I want to touch the soft sand," Charney said, tugging Ruby's pant leg and pointing down the cliff at the rust-red shore.

A wave of irritation rolled over Ruby.

"Soft sand, soft sand, soft sand," Charney cried.

On the other side of Ruby, Layk, Charney's little brother, took up the chant, "soft sand, soft sand."

With a sigh, Ruby took their little hands in hers and led them down the cliff. The sand was soft, but it was also filled with tiny, hooked thorns. The children alternated between playing and crying, and that night Ruby spent hours removing tiny thorns from tiny hands and feet.

When Ruby woke, her hands were cramped, even though that day on the shore was at least a year ago now. The sky outside her window had been replaced with a solid sheet of steel gray cloud. She heard clanging, and the lights in the cabin were flashing. She reached down and shook her comatose roommate. "I think we're here."

The other woman remained still. Ruby got up and threw her bag over her shoulder. She briefly considered brushing her teeth or hair. She left without doing either.

She followed the hallway until she reached the queue of sad women from the class. There were fewer of them than she remembered from orientation. Company employees were going down the line and helping women into puffy, insulated suits and strapping on masks attached to metal canisters on their backs labeled OXYGEN.

Ruby let herself be dressed. It felt kind of nice, relinquishing control and letting someone else do the work. The suit was bulky and heavy, and the mask was pulled so tight she could feel the fat of her cheeks bulging around it. The ensemble was completed with a fitted hood.

"It's going to be cold out there. Hold on tight," the employee said, giving Ruby a small pat on the head before pushing her out of the ship and into a small drone-piloted hovercraft.

As above, so below, Ruby thought as the drone flew her over waves of frozen gray water and chunky gray rocks. She knew it was cold, the Company warned the temperatures outside got down to −85° Fahrenheit, but she couldn't feel anything through the suit.

Ruby gripped the metal pole that stuck out from the center of the hovercraft as hard as she could. Even with her fingers engulfed in the bodysuit, she could feel the blood leaching from them from her death grip. She saw dots, homesteads, well spread out from each other. On a planet 40% larger than Earth, it would probably be some time before she saw anyone else but her Company-issued Companion.

Everything had happened so fast once the children and Dayton had died that she hadn't had time to think about who this new person would be. She had filled out the questionnaire with her preferences. For every personality trait that Dayton had, she picked the opposite. She didn't want anyone who reminded her of him, who would treat her like he treated her, who would do what he did.

Just thinking about him made her hand stray to her neck, to the scar. But the bulky glove hit the cold metal collar that connected her helmet to her suit, instead of soft skin. With a start, she moved her wandering hand back to the pole. She was almost there, to her new life. But without her children, she wasn't sure if she wanted a life at all.

Annie

Annie ran to the airlock controls when she saw the drone approaching. She punched in the sequence to open the first chamber as the small, suited figure clumsily ran for the entrance. When she could see the figure was safely inside, she closed the first lock and opened the second. The drone, seeing its package safely delivered, retreated. Annie felt the familiar squeeze of anxiety she always felt whenever the supply drones retreated, but this time, they weren't leaving her alone. The figure ran into the second chamber and Annie opened the third lock. She went to meet the stranger who was going to be with her 24/7, possibly, for the rest of their lives.

The figure was small and disoriented, and she was tugging at her spacesuit. It must have been impossibly hot, now that she was in the controlled environment of the homestead.

Annie trotted up the lane, past the well-organized rows of growing produce that kept her fed in between supply drop-offs…or would keep them fed if the Company ever forgot they were out here, or abandoned the project without telling them, or went bankrupt, or… She shook the thought out of her head; she needed to think positive thoughts. This first meeting needed to go well.

"Hey, I can help you with that. Hold on," Annie called out.

The figure tore the hood off her head, freeing dark, chin-length hair. She unclipped the mask. "I don't need help." The mask had left angry red marks in an X pattern on her face, but Annie still had to suck in her breath at how beautiful Ruby was.

She took a second to admire Ruby's straight, angry eyebrows, high cheekbones, and elfin ears. But not more than a second, because she could already tell the other woman was annoyed.

Annie put her hands up. "Fine. Just trying to be helpful. You're…"

"Ruby."

"Right. Just let me help you…" Annie reached for the oxygen canisters and Ruby swatted her hands away. The women looked at each other, at an impasse.

"Okay, have it your way."

Ruby shrugged out of the suit and collected it and the canisters.

"That looks heavy."

Ruby glared.

Annie had envisioned offering a tour of the homestead to her new Companion, but she didn't know what to do with this tiny, rage-filled person in front of her. "You must be tired. Can I show you to your room?"

"Sure."

They walked together in silence. *What are we going to do about the rest of our lives?* Annie thought.

Ruby

Ruby tossed and turned in her new room. It was harder to sleep under an alien sky than she thought it would be. She thought longingly of the yellow pills, but she had left the remainder on board the ship. She didn't want to get addicted or be tempted to let her guard down around a stranger.

Annie.

Ruby felt bad, she had been mean to the poor woman. Ruby had stumbled getting off the drone, having underestimated the pull of gravity on her new home planet, and her knees ached. Knowing that the locks and her passage to life were being manned by a stranger hadn't helped her transition to her new home either. The doors could have malfunctioned, or Annie could have been incompetent, and Ruby could have been locked out forever—stranded and dying a slow and painful death.

She didn't think she was so invested in being alive until death loomed over her. She had been hot and panicking trying to get off the suit. It didn't help that Ruby was infuriated as soon as she saw the woman walking toward her. She had specifically requested someone the physical opposite of Dayton. The person walking toward her was pale and freckled, tall with strong forearms, and a shock of strawberry blonde hair which was too close to Dayton's blond for comfort.

Ruby decided to shower before she went down for breakfast. The bathroom was more luxurious than anything she had ever used on Earth. The floor and shower were lined in sunbaked terracotta tiles with real wood accents on the walls. She turned a tap and steam filled the room. She took time scrubbing and buffing like she never had on the trip over. She scrubbed until her skin felt new and raw and pink.

In the bedroom, the wardrobe and dresser were filled with clothes in her size, a present from the Company. *Thank you for giving up the rest of your life to fulfill our company business objectives* she imagined the Company saying, as she slipped them on. They were in her size, to her taste, and practical. She grabbed the tablet the Company assigned her and set off to face her new forever.

Annie was sitting at the marble breakfast bar eating as Ruby descended the staircase. She had her own company-issued tablet out before her. She looked up. "I made you some."

A bowl of oatmeal with strawberries and a cup of steaming coffee was placed opposite Annie. "Thank you," Ruby said. She knew it came out frostier than she intended. What if she didn't take her coffee this way? How could this stranger be so presumptuous?

"The Company told me how you take your coffee," Annie said.

Ruby started, wondering if she had accidentally spoken the thought out loud. Instead, she said, "They really thought of everything, didn't they?"

Annie gave her a wry smile. "They did."

Ruby sat down and turned on the tablet, looking at the assignment for the day. The Company had a rigorous schedule it sent out every day. She imagined it helped keep people sane, as well as on track with their duties. She opened her schedule and scrolled through. The morning started with breakfast with her new Companion, followed by a series of questions they were supposed to ask to "deepen their understanding" of each other. Then calisthenics. Then an introduction to The Work. Then shower. Dinner. Free time. Bedtime. Her whole day, and all the days after, color-coordinated in little boxes.

She didn't have to think or feel if she didn't want to. She could just do. She closed her eyes. When she opened them, Annie looked away quickly. She had been staring at her.

"Does anything happen if you don't follow the schedule?"

"Nah. I just do what I feel like."

"That's kind of scarier, isn't it? Knowing no one cares?"

Annie cocked her head to the side. "I guess it is. I never really thought about it that way. I think they do care that the job is being done. I think they care that we are alive. We are all cogs in the machine, but if one of the cogs malfunctions…it could be over for everyone. At least, that's what they led us to believe."

Ruby considered. Any company investing in the terraforming of a new planet would have backups. Would have backups of backups. Ruby wondered why the Company hadn't hired planet natives and had opted down the must more expensive path of shipping in humans.

"Why do you think this planet is uninhabited?" Ruby asked.

"Who says it's uninhabited?"

Ruby let the question hang. To her, the answer was obvious.

"I do have a few theories," Annie said when she realized Ruby wasn't going to break the silence. "I think maybe they did what we did to our planet. Just messed up the climate and accidentally drove themselves to extinction. Or maybe they are all still here and just exist on a plane we can't understand."

"What do you mean 'can't understand?'"

"Well, we have five senses, right? Six if you believe in that kind of thing. But what about senses we don't have? Can't even imagine? Maybe we are all on top of each other right now, but we can't see or hear or touch or smell them. So, we just…don't know."

Ruby shivered at the thought. "Do you think they can see us?"

"I don't know. But I would feel bad for them if they did." Annie checked her watch. "I guess that fulfills the 'Ask and Answer' part of our itinerary. Do you want to see the gym?"

Ruby crinkled her nose. Annie let out a whoosh of air. "Great. I didn't want to do that either. I just thought you were a rule-follower."

"I used to be. I don't know what I am anymore. I do know I don't want to work out on a stomach full of oatmeal."

"Maybe we could go on that tour?"

Annie showed Ruby around the homestead. Ruby oohed and aahed over the technology that kept the home running safely, efficiently, and at almost 100% no waste. They decided to eschew the schedule for the day and focus on emergency training. Annie showed Ruby how to work the airlocks, the protocols for if their power systems failed, and for if the backup systems failed, what to do if the system went offline, and what do to if the farm's watering and sunlight systems faltered, and they did a few safety runs. By the end of the day, Ruby was exhausted and dripping in sweat.

"I'll take you out to start working on resource collection tomorrow," Annie said, as they ate dinner.

Before bed, Ruby scrolled through the training materials on her tablet. Resource collection was Annie's job for the Company. As Annie's Companion, Ruby wasn't required to work, but she had already made up her mind to help out as much as she could. She wanted a real partnership, like she and Dayton had. Also, the farm was pretty self-sustaining and aside from watching any of the 1000s of entertainment services, she didn't know what else to do to fill her days. So, work it would be.

She read and reread the articles on resource collection procedures until she fell asleep, tablet still in hand, no yellow pills required, and blessedly, no dreams.

Annie

During breakfast, Annie drilled Ruby on the procedures, processes and safety protocols of resource collection. The women decided to blow off their schedule and get right to work. Annie loved being above quota every month, and she didn't want to be slowed down by the disruption of receiving a Companion. They donned their suits and headed out into the cold, gray beyond.

Their first excursion went well—so did their second and third. In retrospect, Annie thought, they were overconfident and that's why things went so wrong. Their fourth time into the field, Ruby broke protocol. Ruby was driving the rover over the frozen sea that lay directly to the southeast of the homestead, with their current load stacked on the back. Annie was in the sidecar, manning the collection arm, when Ruby braked abruptly, and the rover skidded over the ice, sending half the stacked cargo through the dense air.

When the rover came to a stop, Ruby unbuckled herself and jumped off, slipping on the surface of the sea.

The alarm signals started to blare, and Annie could barely hear her own thoughts over the din. She saw Ruby's small figure hunched over, trying to collect the dropped cargo. The pull of gravity was too strong for Ruby to ever budge one of these rocks alone. The robotic arm made collection look easy. Ruby should have known better; the training manual had covered this.

Annie saw Ruby struggling and realized she was stuck. That's when she also broke protocol and jumped out of the sidecar, leaving the rover unmanned. She ran to Ruby and between the two of them, they were able to roll the rock a few millimeters, enough to free Ruby's arm. They turned and started running for the rover, which, detecting it was unmanned, had started to make its way back to the homestead.

In situations where the driver abandoned the craft, it would dock back at the homestead and alert the company. Without the rover, Annie and Ruby would slowly starve and die.

Annie ran harder than she ever had, until she felt her heart would burst. She leaped and found purchase on the lip of the rover. She pulled herself into the driver's seat and slowed it enough for Ruby to hop on. The alarms stopped. It wasn't until after they had docked and gotten safely through all three airlocks that Annie let herself feel anger over her fear.

"You should never, ever have gotten out of that rover."

Ruby pulled off her hood, tears smeared her cheeks. "I'm sorry. I made a mistake."

"You did make a mistake. A huge mistake that could have killed us both."

"I said I'm sorry. What more can I do? Cut off my arm?" Ruby's tears had given way to anger.

"Don't you yell at me, you're the one who messed up. You can't just break protocol because something goes wrong. Things going wrong is exactly why we need protocol. Were you listening to me at all during our trainings?"

"I've studied resource collection," Ruby snapped back. "Just because I'm the Companion and not the Primary doesn't mean I don't know just as much as you do."

"There's a difference between living it and doing it every single day of your life and reading about it, princess. But you'll find that out soon enough."

Ruby reared back as if Annie had slapped her.

"You need to listen to me," Annie said, planting her hands on Ruby's shoulders. "It's not me trying to be controlling or tell you what to do. It's for both of our survival."

"What if I don't care? What if I don't care about survival?"

Annie's mouth dropped open. "What do you mean? Who doesn't care about survival?"

"Don't touch me." Ruby wheeled around on her heel and started back toward the homestead.

Annie didn't see her for the next two days. Much to her surprise, she felt lonely. Lonelier than she had ever felt before Ruby's sudden appearance in her life. She put out coffee and oatmeal with strawberries on it both mornings, in case the other woman came down. On the third morning, Ruby appeared at the breakfast bar. She looked thinner, and her eyes had dark circles underneath them. But Annie's heart leapt when she saw her. She was scared to say the wrong thing. She decided to approach Ruby carefully, like a cat that could bolt at any moment.

"So...you cut off that arm yet?"

Ruby looked up and to Annie's surprise, she laughed. Well, it came out as more of a bark, than a laugh, but Annie decided to count it as a win. "You ready to try again?"

Ruby nodded. "Yeah, let's try again."

The next few weeks passed uneventfully. Annie appreciated Ruby's adherence to protocols, which she interpreted as a gesture of dedication toward rebuilding the trust between them. They needed trust more than they needed anything. In return, Annie started leaving Ruby gifts.

She put ice water in a thermos on Ruby's favorite treadmill before her workouts. She dried mint and put it into little satchels for Ruby to put under her pillow and in her dresser drawers. She left her little notes with corny vintage motivational sayings. "Let's get this bread," read one, "Rise n' grind," said another. She didn't know if Ruby liked them, she never mentioned them, but Annie was hopeful that one day she would.

Trust could blossom into more, couldn't it? Annie didn't know, she had never trusted anyone but herself. She did know she wanted to try.

In time, Ruby started talking again, just a little bit. Every, "How are you?" was a win to Annie. She tried to draw Ruby out of her shell. "Do you want to do a training drill?" "Do you want me to quiz you on farming procedures?" *Do you want? What do you want?*

"You ask me more questions than my kids did," Ruby said after one particularly intense grilling session on the upkeep of their honeybees.

"You have kids?"

"Yeah. I mean, I did."

"What happened to them?" Annie spoke without thinking; she regretted the words as soon as they were out of her mouth.

Ruby's face turned into storm clouds. "I'm going to lie down for a while. I'll see you at dinner."

Annie frantically scrolled through her dossier on Ruby to see if she missed the section where it mentioned Ruby having children. There was nothing there. Meanwhile, there were whole paragraphs on Ruby's personality traits, likes and dislikes, routines and food preferences. Annie swore under her breath. It was just like the Company, to give so much and so little. It did make a little bit of sense; they wanted the couple to get to know each other organically. Laying someone's whole life out on paper, plain as day, would take the mystery out of them. And a little mystery was required to fall in love with someone. After all, who would want to look at the warts before they saw the cute little frog on the other side of those warts.

Not that Ruby was a frog, Annie thought. She was quite beautiful, and the desire to touch her grew stronger every day. But then Annie remembered her yelling, "Don't touch me," and she tucked the desire away.

Ruby

Ruby had lots of regrets. She thought escaping to Keppler 62-F was the solution to her problems, but she just seemed to keep racking regrets up, even here, in the middle of nowhere at the end of the world. She was pushing away the only person she had, and she wasn't a bad person.

Annie was easy on the eyes and easy on her heart. Ruby smiled at the silly notes she left her. She loved inhaling the sweet mint scent as she drifted off to sleep at night. But she didn't know how to stop pushing Annie away. She resolved to tell Annie the truth, the truth that would either bridge the gap between them or make it irreparable.

"I have to tell you something. Something about my past," Ruby said. Annie had made an elaborate dinner for them. There were roasted veggies from the garden and steak from the meat supply the company provided. It would probably go untouched tonight, once she said what she had to say. "Okay. Lay it on me."

"I'm not making excuses for him."

"Making excuses for who?"

"My husband, Dayton. We were starving. There was no food left, no work. No water. No water, no water." She felt herself becoming hysterical. She had been the one to complain about the water. Deep in the most horrible, hidden part of her heart, Ruby knew it was her complaint about the water that had pushed Dayton over the edge. She had never told anyone this before, and everyone who was there was rotting deep in the earth's soil.

She doubled over and drew ragged breaths. "I told him there was no water. I blamed him, I yelled at him. I said he couldn't even provide for his family. I asked him, what right did we have to bring kids into this world? What were we thinking?" Ruby pressed her palms over her eyes, she couldn't bear to look at Annie. "But I didn't mean it. I swear I didn't mean it. I was just scared.

"So, he got up, all quiet. And he got his shotgun. And he shot me here," Ruby pointed at the scar at her collarbone, "and here." She pointed at her stomach. "I wasn't even a moving target, because I didn't think he was really going to do it. It didn't even really hurt, it just felt warm and wet. I fell, and I heard more shots and screams. Then everything was quiet. For a long time. I woke up in a medical bay and they gave me some choices. I chose this. That's how I got here. Are you happy you know?"

Annie closed the space between them. She took Ruby's hands and held them to her heart. "Listen to me, none of that was your fault. It's a hard life on Earth. It's a hard life here. People do crazy things when survival is on the line. Look at us."

Ruby laughed through her tears. "We are crazy."

"We are. And we do what we have to do to survive."

"I don't know why I want to live. How can I want to go on without them?"

"Your death won't bring them back. It won't bring them peace. But going on, and living, will expand the capacity in your heart for joy. And your children can live there. Dayton can live there. Maybe I can live there too."

Annie

Annie let the heaviness of the moment settle over them. She guided Ruby's hands to her waist and placed her arms around the smaller woman's shoulders. She leaned in and placed her dry cheek against Ruby's wet one. She didn't dare to breathe. She felt Ruby relax into her. And then. Finally. Salty lips against hers. A kiss, an opening, a beginning.

From the Author

As someone obsessed with sci-fi and post-apocalypse fiction, I think a lot about why I, and the public as a whole, are so captivated by the prospect of a mass event altering our way of life forever. And I think it's because we have all experienced something similar to this, but on a personal scale. The one big, often horrible, event that irrevocably changes us and our view of the world and ourselves.

"The *Company* We Keep" is a treatise on grief, how it changes us, how we learn to live with it, and how the human spirit always moves toward survival and love, no matter how impossible it may seem.

I hope that anyone who has suffered through their own personal apocalypse can find happiness again and maybe even a bit of hope or comfort in the story of Annie and Ruby.

About the Author

Natasia Langfelder is a born and bred Brooklynite. You can find her work in *The Threepenny Review*, OffLimits Press, Sirens Call Publications, Cloaked Press, Papers Publishing, Wicked Shadows Press, and more.

When she's not writing, you can find her on the couch with her partner and their teacup yorkie. To keep up with her work, follow her on:
Instagram @lady_misfortune_
or
Twitter @natasiarose.

Falling

by
A.M. Burns

Falling

Hercaleon loved the Valley of the Mists. In a lot of ways, it was preferable to living in Dragon Hill in Lestian. The massive waterfall at the north end of the valley provided the never-ending mists that gave the valley its name. High cliff walls provided ample, magically-carved caves for the dragons and their riders to make home in.

"How soon before we can hunt?" Chromath, Hercaleon's blue dragon, asked through their mental link as he swooped into the mist.

"I need to check in first, then we can hunt." Hercaleon patted Chromath's neck. The bright sun on the flight from the last portal to the valley had left Chromath's hide warm to the touch.

"Don't take too long." Chromath backwinged and landed on the lush grass just down from the path leading to the trainer's cave.

When Chromath crouched, Hercaleon undid his riding straps, swung out of the saddle, and jumped off Chromath's foreleg to land gracefully next to his dragon. Chromath was the largest blue dragon of his hatch. Sometimes, after hours in the saddle, Hercaleon, and his knees, wished for a slightly shorter mount. He'd never wished for one of the larger colors, like brown, or red. A small, agile blue was as big as he wanted.

Besides Trainer Geral's blue dragon, Felmar, there weren't any other dragons playing in the river or sunning themselves on their shelves outside the trainees' caves.

The path up to the trainer's cave was short and not nearly as steep as most of the other paths from the valley floor to the caves. Hercaleon welcomed the opportunity to stretch his legs, even for just a little bit.

"Greetings, Felmar." Hercaleon gave a short bow when he reached the cave, as was proper when greeting a dragon who was higher in the flight's pecking order than his own.

Felmar gave him a brief bow.

"Stop talking to him and get in here, Boy," a gravelly voice rumbled from the cave. It was impossible to not recognize Geral's tones.

During the two years Hercaleon had been in the valley learning the finer points of being a dragon rider, and growing Chromath to his impressive size, he'd learned the hard way to follow every order the trainer gave.

Walking past Felmar, Hercaleon made his way into the cave. There wasn't anyone in the open chamber between the shelf and the bedchamber. Papers covered the central table, but that was the only sign of anyone inhabiting the place.

"I'm back here." Something tapped on the stone floor, drawing Hercaleon's attention toward the bedchamber.

There was a faint light coming through the opening separating the two spaces. Someone had pulled aside the hide that normally hung across the opening.

Geral sat in his bed. He was propped up on several cushions and had his feet stretched out. One foot was wrapped in a splint, as was one arm. The arm was strapped across his broad hairy chest. "Took you long enough to get here. Did that messenger take the long route and poke the Sielew?"

"No, sir." Hercaleon shook his head. He hadn't heard of any new conflicts with the invaders, who were hell bent on taking over Lestian from the people who'd held it for more generations than he could count. "I was out on patrol on the Northern coast."

"Those're dangerous lands." Geral nodded. "Are things still quiet at home?"

"Yes, sir. There haven't been any attacks in months. We believe that during the last battle we devastated their pegasi flight, but the priests' defenses remain strong. There are also rumors that they're working on new treaties with the Silver Queen for weapons."

"We desperately need allies in this war." Geral closed his eyes and stroked his long black beard with his good hand.

"He's talking too much. I'm hungry," Chromath complained.

Hercaleon forced himself not to smile. "Sir, what happened? Your message only said you'd been injured and needed help while you heal." He waved at the trainer's right side. "The injury is obvious."

Geral frowned as he opened his eyes. "One of the new riders has trouble controlling their mount. To be honest, we were trying something a little complex. We were too close to the ground.

Felmar didn't have time to react and get his fat butt to me in time." Geral growled. "Yes, your butt is fat!"

A deep huff came from the shelf beyond the sitting chamber.

"Anyway. I hit the ground hard. I had to send one of the trainees to the Bastette village and get a healer to come lend me a hand." He shifted in the bed and grimaced. "I need you to cover for me for a month or so. It would be nice if fast healing was one of the gifts we get from our dragons."

Like every dragon rider, Hercaleon was well aware of the limits of the gifts they gained from bonding with the dragons. They might be stronger, faster, and many other things, but they still took time to heal. A low-altitude fall was one thing all riders dreaded.

"Where are they now?" Hercaleon pointed out of the cave, knowing Geral would understand he meant the trainees.

"Hunting. They should be back soon. If Chromath wants to hunt, as long as you don't go far, you should have time." A sly smile darkened Geral's face. "I told them to go find some pachyphants. The last herds I saw were a good hour flight away. And they're supposed to bring back enough for Felmar."

Hercaleon arched an eyebrow. "Are their dragons large enough for that yet?"

"Yes, if they think to break them up and don't try to carry more than half of one each." Geral snorted.

"So, it's going to take them more than an hour to come back, after they bring down enough pachyphants to feed everyone." Hercaleon wondered how many times during his own training had Geral come up with something like that to keep the flight busy.

"Exactly." Geral pointed down and to the south. "The old blacksmith cave is still open. Use it while you're here."

Hercaleon bowed. "I remember it. I'll check in with you after I get Chromath fed and settled in."

"If you want to go find the trainees, you're welcome to. They might need some help getting enough food back." Geral snorted again.

Turning on his heel, Hercaleon headed out of the cave.

On his way out, he gave another bow to Felmar. "We'll be back with some food in a bit."

Chromath met him at the foot of the ramp, standing close enough to the trail that Hercaleon didn't need to go all the way down. He easily swung into the saddle and fastened his flight straps as Chromath bunched up his haunches and then launched himself into the misty sky.

"He talks too much." Chromath cleared the valley rim with just a few wing beats and headed south.

"Can you find the trainees?" Hercaleon scanned the sky for any sign of them, but sometimes blue dragons were hard to spot in a cloudless blue sky. That was one of the reasons they had the largest clutches of any color of dragons in Lestian.

"Maybe, after I eat. Pachyphants are a little tougher than I want to eat right now."

Hercaleon laughed. "You love pachyphant, and you know it. Weren't you complaining the other day that you haven't had pachyphant in years?"

"Maybe. Was I awake?" Chromath turned on a wing tip and headed east, crossing the river.

"Where are you going?" Hercaleon put his hand above his eyes and scanned the horizon. There was a bit of dust just ahead of them.

"There's a herd of zekbra. They're almost as tasty as pachyphant."

Something moved in the sky above the dust cloud. Darker specks, that Hercaleon had to really focus on to make out as they circled something.

"Is that the flight?"

Chromath tilted his head. *"Maybe. They don't have any pachyphants if it is. Felmar won't be happy if he doesn't get his pachyphant today."*

"Then Felmar can go get his own pachyphant." Hercaleon leaned forward, straining his riding straps and his eyes. The flight looked to be about thirty strong. "See if they respond to you."

After a moment, Chromath huffed. *"Yes, that's them. The lead had the audacity to ask who I was."*

"The last time you saw them, they were still waddling across the hatching sands in Dragon Hill." Hercaleon settled back in his saddle. "I doubt you tried to make much of an impression on them at that time."

"And why would I? Too many of them don't survive training."

It was the hard truth about being a dragon rider. So many, no matter which color of dragon they rode, didn't make it out of training. Accidents were common, and Geral was the first time

Hercaleon knew of anyone finding a healer for an injury in the valley. Back at Dragon Hill, there were several healers, but most of the times when a dragon rider got injured, he died. Injuries several thousand feet in the air were fatal. They all knew that.

"The zekbra are the first prey they've spotted since they left the valley," Chromath relayed.

"Then it's a good thing you didn't have your heart set on pachyphant." Hercaleon laughed and patted Chromath's neck. Even after the long ride from the portal, it was good to be in the saddle and hunting the lands around the Valley of Mists. "Let's show them how to do this."

A subtle chuckle rumbled through Chromath, shaking Hercaleon's legs. *"Of course."* The blue dragon tucked his wings and dropped out of the sky.

The zekbra herd was large, easily thirty to forty animals. They ran, abandoning the grass for the rocky transition land that would eventually turn into desert in a few miles. A couple of them split north, while the rest of the herd headed south, toward the jungle where their black and white stripes would give them more camouflage than just running in a herd did.

"Hold on. I've got one." Chromath pumped his wings, heading for one of the larger beasts running north.

Someone shouted, "Help!" above them.

Hercaleon craned his neck around, trying to see what was happening. "Chromath. What's going on?"

"Some trainee fell off their dragon. No big deal." He extended his front legs, flexing his talons, ready to grab the zekbra.

"Chromath, we have to catch them." For the first time in hours, Hercaleon snatched up his reins and jerked.

"Damnit." Chromath shot up, flapping his wings hard to get altitude. *"You made me miss that one. Now one of the youngsters will get it."*

"Someone's in trouble." Hercaleon still couldn't spot the falling rider. "We need to save them. The food will still be around after we do." For the years the war with the Sielew had been going on, they never seemed to have enough dragons or riders to adequately protect their territory. Every dragon and rider was important. This batch was almost done with their training; too much time and resources had gone into them to let one die on his watch.

"There he is." Hercaleon sent an image of the cloud formation above the trainee to give Chromath something to go on.

Several other dragons were franticly trying to reach him, including one without a rider.

"Call the others off." Hercaleon shook his head. Didn't these trainees know better than to risk mid-air collisions by having too many dragons in a tight space?

"We could catch all of them if you want." Chromath sighed.

Seconds later the other dragons, except for the riderless one, peeled off, resuming the hunt.

"Chromath, show him how to do it. Tell him to show his rider." There was still enough space for the dragon to rescue his rider. If they were in battle, the odds were another rider wouldn't be able to stop fighting long enough to help. Dragons and riders had to work as teams.

The rider flattened out, spreading his arms and legs like a skinned and drying pelt. His rate of decent slowed.

Swooping in, the dragon went past him once. Closer, the dragon slowed, then spread his wings as he angled toward the rider.

For a moment, the rider disappeared from view.

A loud whoop came from that direction.

The dragon banked, and the rider was visible in the saddle.

"Tell them to land. Now." Hercaleon held on as Chromath headed toward the rocky land below them.

"Can this wait until we get back to the valley? I haven't killed anything yet."

"No. We handle things when things come up." It was one of the things Geral had drilled into his head during his own training. If there's a problem, address it instantly, while it was still fresh in everyone's mind. If the rider had been goofing off while flying, that was inexcusable.

Chromath landed on a boulder, and the other dragon landed next to him. The dragon was not quite two years old yet, so even if Chromath had been average for his age, the youngling was still only half the size of the full-grown blue dragon. The rider, on the other hand, was a little tall for a trainee.

"Wow, so that's how that's supposed to work. I never really got it when Geral tried to explain it. But then he never had Felmar explain to Lukeom to show me. That makes sense. Thanks." The rider chattered more than Hercaleon expected.

"What happened up there?" Hercaleon wasn't in the mood for dancing around things.

The rider fiddled with one of his straps, and then held it up. "This." The strap looked like it had been cut partially through. "Somebody tried to kill me."

A chill, like a frozen knife, sliced through Hercaleon. Riders might have issues with one another, but they were forbidden from attacking each other. Their dragons shouldn't have allowed something like this to happen. Didn't they know the rules, or did they just not care? "Did you fail to check your gear before you left the valley this morning?"

"No." The rider pulled off his blue helmet and ran a shaking hand through his short black hair. "Everything was fine when we left this morning. If we'd been in battle, I'd swear an arrow nicked it instead of me, but we weren't. We've been in the air most of the day looking for prey and there's none that we can find. With the storms coming up from the south, we figured everything's hiding."

"Storms?" Hercaleon twisted in his saddle and stared to the south. The horizon looked darker than it should've. Something big was moving their way.

"Yeah. Storms." The trainee cocked his head. "We should probably get these zekbras down and head to the valley."

"We've got just enough time." Chromath stomped his foot. *"And I'm not going to get to hunt."*

Hercaleon patted his neck. "Tomorrow. If this storm blows out by then. Hopefully the others have taken out enough for you and Felmar to share."

"I hate sharing." Chromath turned his head back and glared.

The trainee next to them turned and winced.

"What's wrong?" Hercaleon shook his head, hoping the day wasn't getting worse by the minute.

"My hip hurts. I wrenched my leg when the strap failed, and I tried to keep from falling."

"Chromath. Tell the other dragons to pick up what they can carry, and get a little for Felmar, and fly back to the valley. I need to look into this and see what we need to do."

"I need to eat."

"You're not going to starve." Hercaleon undid his saddle straps and then slid down Chromath's side to land on the rocks. It would've been better to be in the grass, but he wanted to make sure the rider didn't have anything broken.

"Here." Hercaleon reached up for the rider. "Let me help you down, and then we can get a better look at this."

"Thanks." The young man had a strong grip in his large hands.

With the way his bond with Chromath augmented his strength, Hercaleon easily lifted the young man down and set him on the uneven ground with his legs out in front of him.

Above them, the rest of the flight flew, burdened with as much meat as they could carry. One of the riders, on a midsized dragon, glared in their direction for a moment.

"Chromath, if there's leftovers, you and Lukeom head over and eat quickly. We need to be out of here before the storm hits."

"*Finally.*" Chromath launched first.

Lukeom put his head on his rider's for a moment.

The rider laughed and patted his snout. "I'll be fine. Go eat." There was the softness that most dragon riders reserved for their mounts.

The young dragon fixed his gaze on Hercaleon. Although he couldn't hear the thoughts, the meaning was clear.

"I'll make sure he's fine." Hercaleon touched the dragon's muzzle. He rarely made such a move. Most dragons didn't like to be touched by other people, even other riders. But Lukeom pushed against Hercaleon's hand for a moment, then blew out a bit of hot breath before taking off to follow Chromath.

Hercaleon looked at the rider. "What's your name?"

"Oh, yeah. Abu. I'm Abu." He smiled and a bit of color flushed his cheeks.

"I'm Hercaleon. I'm going to be filling in for Geral until he's back on his feet."

Abu sighed and stared at his hands in his lap. "I'm really sorry for what happened to him. Lukeom and I tried to catch him, but he just fell. It was almost like his saddle straps had been cut."

That wasn't something Hercaleon wanted to think about. "You're the one involved in the accident?"

"Most of us were." Abu didn't look up. "But Lukeom and I were the ones who hit him last."

As much as Hercaleon wanted to know more, he shook his head. "Let's talk about that more back in the valley. Now, let's take a look at your hip." Hercaleon again reached for Abu. "I'll help you stand, then lean against the boulder here, so I can get a look under the leathers."

Abu grasped Hercaleon's hands and he hauled him up and then turned a little so Abu could be in the right position against the boulder.

"Damn." Abu closed his eyes. "This hurts."

"Hold on a bit longer." Hercaleon undid Abu's belt and the laces holding his leathers closed. Like most Lestians, he knew a little bit about first aid. People who'd been at war for years picked up little things to help them stay alive. "Now, tell me what hurts worst." Hercaleon felt Abu's muscular thigh and then up his side.

Abu jumped. "There," he forced out through gritted teeth.

"Okay." Hercaleon pressed more, trying to ignore the way Abu jumped and whined when he hit tender spots. The pain seemed to be localized in the hip joint but there didn't seem to be any disconcerting lumps or oddness in the joint.

After comparing both sides, he looked up into Abu's handsome face. Tears ran down the young man's cheeks and into his short beard. "I don't think you've broken anything. I think it's just sprained. But I'm not a healer."

"There's one in the Bastette village," Abu offered.

Hercaleon pulled Abu's leathers back into place. The younger rider jumped again when they got the leathers over his narrow hips. "Going there will be Geral's call." He wasn't going to upset the trainer more than he could help, particularly not on his first day helping out.

"The storm's getting close," Chromath advised. *"We're about done eating. I don't like having to settle for so much zekbra backside."*

"Then the two of you get back here so we can get back to the valley." Hercaleon looked at Abu. "Think you can handle the flight back?"

Abu leaned heavily against the boulder. "I think so. If you can get me back into my saddle."

"I think I can make that happen." Hercaleon looked up as Chromath and Lukeom flew toward them. *"Let Lukeom land first, once they're in the air, I can mount."*

"We'd better move quickly." Chromath circled them as Lukeom landed gracefully next to the boulder.

Abu patted Lukeom's neck. "See, I told you I'd be okay. Hercaleon's going to help me mount."

Lukeom got as low as he could. Luckily, he was still short enough that Hercaleon, doing his best to not put too much pressure on the injured hip, was able to lift Abu up.

"Okay." Again, Abu's teeth were gritted against the pain.

"Take it easy on the take off." Hercaleon patted Lukeom on the shoulder, then touched Abu's leg. "See you back in the valley."

"Right." Abu nodded.

Lukeom took off.

Abu screamed, falling forward in the saddle.

"Chromath?" Hercaleon's heart stopped beating for a moment.

"Lukeom says he might not look stable, but he's not moving strangely in the saddle."

That wasn't exactly reassuring. *"Does he think he can make it to the valley?"* If he had to carry Abu on the front of Chromath's saddle, he could, but it would slow them down and they might get caught by the storm.

"Yes." Chromath swooped toward Hercaleon.

"Tell him we'll catch up." As he waited for Chromath to land so he could mount, Hercaleon couldn't help but wonder what kind of mess Geral had gotten him into with this new flight.

The clouds were thick, but the sky above them was clear blue. Hercaleon relaxed in the saddle as Chromath leveled out in the cooler upper air. When he'd headed to the Valley of Mists, he'd forgotten it was the rainy season, but that hadn't stopped him from working the trainees. Sure, they never had to worry about a major assault from Sielew during a storm—their pegasi didn't fly at all with wet feathers—but it was good for dragon riders to know the obstacles they might face if caught out in a downpour.

The trainee flight was called Lapis Flight, he'd been informed when he asked. Each hatching group had its own flight name. He and Chromath had been part of Azure flight. There were only a few of them left. Blue dragons took a lot more casualties than the others. Being smaller and more maneuverable, they were more active during battle.

"Tell them all to fan out in a wide V formation." Hercaleon wanted to make sure the trainees at least knew that much. He'd been working them for Geral for almost two weeks and was still finding holes in their training.

"They're working on it." Chromath snorted, as unamused as Hercaleon about the lack of basic knowledge.

"Order Lukeom to take point. He's the biggest, he's in charge." Hercaleon shook his head. How could such a core piece of training have slipped through the whole flight? It was a very basic dragon idea that stopped nearly all fights, at least between dragons. The biggest guy was in charge. Plain and simple.

Hercaleon watched while the trainees adjusted themselves into the proper formation. It took them a couple of minutes, but they managed to pull it off.

"Let's disappear into the clouds." Hercaleon grinned mischievously. He'd always hated it when Geral pulled this move on his flight during training.

A chuckle rumbled through Chromath as he did a flawless wingover and arrowed into the clouds. *"I'll tell them to find us."*

"Right." Hercaleon sighed as Chromath leveled out but stayed inside the cloud. It was thick and cold there. Already being soaked to the bone from flying through the storm to get into the cloud had been rough, but flying in the cloud itself was even more chilling. Ice had started forming on Hercaleon's mustache by the time he'd had enough.

"They've lost us, haven't they?"

"It appears so," Chromath agreed.

"Then let's see if we can pick a couple of them off. Shall we?" Hercaleon grabbed the front of his saddle and held on as Chromath changed directions and flew up. They came up in the middle of the wing.

Thirty dragons flew around them, still in their V formation, which was good. But Chromath's sudden appearance seemed to take most of them by surprise.

"Take your pick." Hercaleon patted Chromath's shoulder as they cleared the flight and Chromath swung around for their attack.

They were high enough he didn't worry about any riders actually hitting the ground.

Chromath angled toward one of the dragons in the middle part of the left arm of the V. He came in hot and fast, snatching the rider out of the saddle, and then throwing her through the air.

The dragon roared, came at Chromath, only to turn on its tail and fly frantically to catch its rider.

"We hated this game, but I can see how it's fun now." Chromath flew up a couple of wingbeats, then dove for his next target.

The flight broke and scattered around them. That was exactly what they were supposed to do. Avoid a larger attacker, then come in and try to rid the mount of its rider. Chromath was twice—almost three times—the size of a Sielew pegasus. He made an easier target, but also provided his rider more protection. At least the riders didn't have priests hurling balls of hellfire at them while they dealt with an aerial foe.

Chromath spun on his tail and dove out of the way of three dragons determined to catch him. He managed to get close enough to one, to remove the rider, and thus the dragon from the game. They skimmed the upper surface of the clouds, trying to confuse the trainees even more.

Hercaleon grinned as they swooped up, going through the midst of the trainees and scattering them even more. What would his life be like if he managed to follow in Geral's footsteps and took over as trainer when Geral was either retired or was killed in battle? He might really enjoy working the new riders.

A flash of blue was his only warning. Dragon talons wrapped around his torso and yanked him out of his straps and saddle. His legs and hips ached from the rough handling.

"I guess I win!" Abu shouted above him.

Chromath roared and slammed into Lukeom from below.

Lukeom lost his grip on Hercaleon, sending him tumbling head over heels across the sky.

Seconds later, Abu flew past him.

"I've got you." Chromath came in below Hercaleon as he got himself leveled out.

When Chromath spread his wings and glided up just enough. Hercaleon grabbed hold of his saddle and pulled himself back into his seat. "Hold steady." Hercaleon quickly undid his riding straps, then fastened them back in place, a little tighter than normal so he didn't get yanked out again.

Hercaleon couldn't help but grin. He'd always wanted to pull a stunt like that on Geral but had never worked up the nerve to do it. Since Hercaleon had arrived in the valley, Abu had been pushing the boundaries with him. From what he'd heard, he'd pushed Geral too, but not to the same extent.

"All the dragons have caught their riders." Chromath put on a little altitude.

"Then let's head to the plains, see if we can get out of the storms for a bit and do some hunting." Hercaleon wanted to get out of the rain and enjoy dry flying for a bit. They also needed the meat.

Chromath turned on his wing tip and headed south. *"Everyone's falling in behind us."* He'd taken lead, as was his right.

Hercaleon stretched out by the river and watched as Chromath and the other dragons ate their fill of the small herd of pachyphants they'd found. The huge gray beasts with long, strange noses had been easy for Chromath and Lukeom to bring down, but the smaller dragons had a bit of difficulty with such large prey. After a good high-flying training day, a successful hunt was what he needed, and he knew the trainees would feel better when their dragons had full bellies.

Abu plopped down next to Hercaleon and pulled off his helmet. "That's what Geral was supposed to do when he got hurt, wasn't it."

"What?" Hercaleon turned to look at Abu. The late afternoon light made his black hair almost a deep blue. "Have you all been up high enough?"

"Should we have been up high like we just were?"

Hercaleon nodded. "Yeah, that works a lot better for flight training than low flying. Sure, there's not as far to fall, but there's less time for a dragon to catch you."

"Then why is he keeping us low?"

Why indeed? Hercaleon scratched his beard. "I'll ask him about that. Has he never taken you all up above the clouds?" It was another thing that felt wrong.

Abu shook his head. "We always stay below cloud level. Even when there aren't any clouds. He says that the pegasi don't fly very high."

"They don't if there's clouds, but on a cloudless day, you have to worry about their attacks from above as well as below." Hercaleon frowned. What all had Geral and Felmar failed to teach the riders and their dragons? Was the Lapis Flight going to be as effective as older flights when it came to protecting the larger dragons and attacking their Sielew foes?

"That's what I thought. I've seen some of the battles from my father's tower." Abu set his flight helmet behind him and stretched out next to Hercaleon in the grass.

"Father's tower? You're an elite?" Hercaleon didn't know of any Lestians except the elite class who had their own towers. Many of the elites were mages, and they used the towers to help defend people during battles above the city.

"Yeah." Abu nodded. "But I don't have any magic. A real disappointment to my family. Right after my father gave up on ever milking any magic out of me when I turned twenty, it was announced they needed volunteers for a hatching. I jumped at the chance to get away from my dad. Mages and dragons don't mix. That's good for me." He raised up on an elbow and stared toward where the dragons were feasting. "I think bonding with Lukeom was the most incredible thing I've ever done. It's better than magic if you ask me."

"I'm common born, but yeah, I think dragons are better than magic."

Dragon riders came from all of the various quarters of Lestian; most of them just didn't fit where they'd been born, for one reason or another. Talking too much about life before being bonded was frowned upon. Dragon riders were dragon riders and that was it.

"Dragons make us all equal." Abu stared up at the sky. "There's a lot about being a dragon rider that I didn't expect. Like the equal part. Having to do everything for myself. That took some adjusting. But Lukeom makes it all worth it. Now that we're flying, it's even better. That first year, until he was big enough to carry me, was hard."

"As long as he doesn't end up injured, you don't have to worry about that again." Hercaleon wasn't sure what he'd do if Chromath was ever grounded. Flying was just too much fun.

"Or if I don't get injured." Abu sighed. "I'm still sorry that Geral got hurt. I didn't think he would."

"I'm full," Chromath announced. *"I'm going to just lie in the river for a while."*

"Enjoy yourself." Hercaleon turned a little so he could look Abu in the face. The sun was still making the younger rider's hair blue. "Has Geral showed you all how to skin and tan hides yet, or what parts to keep for trade?"

Abu nodded. "Yeah. Skinning these guys is a pain unless the dragons helped do it before eating."

Hercaleon pursed his lips and sighed. "I should've thought of that at the end of the hunt. But there's still enough hide on most of these to be able to get some smaller skins that we can sell."

"Then we don't need to sit here too long." Abu sat straight and looked around. "Looks like some of the riders are napping too."

"If we nap too long, it's going to be dark before we get back to the valley." Hercaleon straightened.

Abu bumped his shoulder and grinned. "Then we'd better get these beasts skinned and set aside some meat for Felmar. You know he never stayed as close to Geral as he has since the accident."

"Dragons worry about us as much as we do them. When something like this happens, they start realizing we're more delicate, and they worry more." Hercaleon got to his feet and offered a hand up to Abu. Although it had been a short time, it had felt nice just sitting in the grass talking. So many of his flight had died in the war. It had been a while since he had someone to just talk to.

"So, I have to keep him from worrying, by keeping myself in one piece." Abu kept hold of Hercaleon's hand a little longer than he needed to.

"Exactly. You're a team."

Abu turned loose of Hercaleon's hand. "We're all a team. A flight. Lapis Flight!" He pumped his fist in the air.

Around them, the other riders lifted their fists and shouted, "Lapis Flight."

Tym, whose dragon was Nyke, didn't join in. He shot a dark look in their direction, then stomped off toward the closest carcass as he pulled out his knife.

Unbothered by what one trainee felt, Hercaleon grinned at the group's strengthening camaraderie. He was starting to wish he'd been there longer, so he knew more of them and their dragons better. "Alright, all of you, get these beasts skinned so we can get back to the valley before nightfall." With Abu at his side, Hercaleon headed to the closest carcass and set to work, thankful the dragon who'd eaten part of it, had done so delicately so they could salvage the hide and tusks. It was good that Geral had taught this flight some things. The problem was there were too many things he hadn't.

The blacksmith's old quarters hadn't been used in years. It had taken Hercaleon, with Chromath hauling things from the entrance, several days to make it livable, and still he wished there was a spot farther up the canyon he could stay. The only plus to the place was it was close to the river for Chromath to enjoy his morning swim and Hercaleon to enjoy his evening one.

"Someone's coming," Chromath muttered sleepily from the wide patio that was similar to the shelf he was used to back in Dragon Hill. *"They don't have their dragon, so I'm not sure who. You can deal with it."*

That Chromath thought he could deal with anything the trainees could dish out was reassuring. Hercaleon swam over to a rock on the bank and hauled himself out of the water. His clothes and knife were within reach.

Abu stepped out of the moon shadows and started toward the water's edge.

Hercaleon cleared his throat.

"Oh." Abu stopped and spun toward him. "I'm sorry. I didn't mean to disturb you, Hercaleon."

"I figured everyone had already called it a night, after the long flight back with the meat and skins."

"I thought a nice swim before bed would help me sleep. Lukeom is already sleeping off his full belly, and everyone in my cave is snoring loudly." He shook his head. "So much loud snoring. Look, if you want time to yourself, I can go."

It was tempting, but in the past couple of weeks, Hercaleon had found them crossing paths more and more often. Like their earlier discussion after the hunt, he enjoyed most of their interactions. "No, I was about done. Go ahead and enjoy yourself."

"You're sure?" Abu sat on the rock just a short distance from Hercaleon. "I really don't mind. If I pull my pillow over my ears, I can muffle some of the snoring."

Hercaleon laughed. "I'm common born, from a large family; I know that doesn't work. Wait until Lukeom is large enough to snore, you'll never get any sleep."

"I'm an only child." Abu ran his finger along the rock thoughtfully. "That's why my father tried so hard to draw magic out of me. He doesn't have anyone else to carry on the family name after I'm gone. My mother died in one of the Sielew attacks when I was young, and he could never bring himself to remarry. True love and all that."

"I lost a sister to an attack." Hercaleon lay back and put his hands behind his head. "By now, who knows, they might all be dead. All I know is none of the rest of them bonded with a dragon; if they had, I'd know."

"Is that why you volunteered to be a dragon rider?" Abu pulled his tunic off, folded it, and put it on the rock behind him. "Your sister, I mean? To help you get revenge on Sielew for the war they've fought with us?"

Hercaleon shook his head. "No. There weren't many other options when I signed up. I was a little younger than you were. I'd just turned sixteen. My folks were having a hard time of it with too many mouths to feed. I just couldn't find a way to bring in money to help out. Nobody was looking for apprentices at the time. Winter was setting in, so there was no work in the fields. The hatching happened and I hoped I'd have a place to stay warm and food to eat."

"And if we can stay alive, we have that." Pulling his trousers down, Abu finished the sentence for him. "How hard is it, really, to stay alive when you're in a battle? Geral has tales, but I'm not sure I believe all of his tales."

"Depends on what you mean by hard." Hercaleon shrugged, wishing they had a bottle of pomegranate wine they could split while they talked. "The biggest thing is to trust Lukeom. Your dragon will do whatever is needed to keep you alive. Beyond that, learn to watch everything around you. Don't react to things, but act on them."

"Geral says that all the time, and I don't totally understand." Abu folded up his trousers and laid them on top of his tunic, then sat on the pile, pulling his knees up and resting his head on them.

"Today, when we were up over the clouds, you didn't scream or flail around like you did the first day I was here and your strap broke."

"It was cut. But I remembered what you had Chromath tell Lukeom about me getting flat in the air to try to slow down and give Lukeom more time to reach me."

"Right." Hercaleon had Chromath talking with the other dragons to try to figure out who'd cut it, but so far, his mount wasn't having a lot of luck. Riders could lie to other riders, but dragons couldn't lie to other dragons. "That first day, you reacted. You screamed and panicked. Today you acted. You got flat, had a little control of your falling speed, and waited for your dragon." He pointed up to the starry sky. "When you're up there, if you react, and that action is wrong, you're more likely to panic. If you stop, and purposely act on something, it's more likely going to be what saves your life, or the life of your dragon."

"I can see that." Abu nodded. "Some of the younger riders just do things without thinking about them."

"And they're more apt to get hurt."

"Have you thought about being trainer here? You're better at it than Geral. At least I think so, and trust me, I've had a lot of magical teachers over the years; the good, the bad, and the horrible. Geral's not bad, but you're better."

Hercaleon shrugged again. "It's not that easy. When there's not a blue hatching, Geral's back in Dragon Hill, being a blue rider with the rest of us. If there're riders and dragons to train, he's here. Maybe when Geral's gone, and if Chromath is the biggest blue dragon at the time, I might get offered the post."

"Everything with the dragons really does just involve size." Abu shook his head. "I guess that makes things easier in some ways."

"It does. The red dragons are above everyone, and Warlord Tygar leads the riders because his red, Brombredir, leads the dragons—because he's the biggest." Hercaleon flashed back to a battle where the Azure Wing was protecting Brombredir, and how they struggled to keep up with the massive dragon's flight and at the same time fought off the pegasi attacking him. He shivered. It had been a big fight, and they'd lost a lot of riders and dragons. Not just blues but all colors. Standing, Hercaleon then jumped as far as he could into the river. The warm water closed in over him. It wasn't like anything he'd encountered in the skies. He felt safe.

Abu plunged in after him.

"Are you okay?" Chromath asked sleepily. *"If he's bothering you, I can wake Lukeom and tell him to handle his rider."*

"I'm fine." Hercaleon was a little surprised that Abu had followed him into the water.

They surfaced at the same time.

"What happened?" Abu asked. "You were talking about dragons, then jumped in. Am I bothering you?"

Hercaleon shook his head, splashing water into Abu's face. "No. I just suddenly remembered one of the bad battles. Where we lost a lot of good riders." Treading water. He took a deep breath. "I'd like to talk about something else."

Abu bobbed in front of him, the moonlight glistened off the water droplets on his eyelashes. "Do you like me?"

Heat rose in Hercaleon's face. "What's not to like?" It came out a dumb response. Hercaleon knew what Abu was asking. He wasn't unknowing in the ways of pleasure. Dragon riders had different thoughts about it than other Lestians. So much of their life was controlled by their dragons. Physical pleasure was often pushed on them. When dragons mated, so did their riders. Other times riders came together to let off steam or relax after a battle. Anything was possible.

"You caught my eye that first day." Abu put his hand on Hercaleon's shoulder. "I'm not sure if you have someone back at Dragon Hill or not."

Hercaleon shook his head. "Nothing permanent."

"Good." Abu drew him closer, and their lips met.

"Oh, this again." Chromath grumbled. The impression of Chromath tucking his head under his wing was loud and clear.

Smiling against Abu's lips, Hercaleon gave himself over to the man in his arms, kicking his legs just enough to keep them bobbing along in the river.

Hercaleon leaned against the stone wall of Geral's bedchamber and watched as the Bastette healer looked at the trainer's wounds. The dark-skinned woman hummed as she rewrapped the bandages on his leg.

"At least it appears you have been listening to my recommendations and staying off the leg as much as possible. Maybe next week you can begin limited walking." She finished wrapping the bandage, cut off the end, and attached it with a strange, bent pin. "Now, about my payment."

Geral's eyes grew large. "You never mentioned payment before."

"Do you think we provide you with our valley and then my services and don't expect something in return?" The woman put the remainer of the bandages in her reed basket. "Especially when your dragons are eating so many animals around here. I require compensation. Do I need to send our chief to have a word with your warlord?"

"No." Geral shook his head. "What do you want?"

"Ivory. Some of the tusks from the pachyphants you slew would be fine." She slung the basket across her narrow shoulders and tugged on the brightly colored, woven straps to make it settle. "And maybe some of the hides as well."

Geral glared at her. "Fine. Whatever. It might be time I get the warlord down here to renegotiate our agreement anyway. I'm sure there are other tribes who would be interested in leasing us land."

She nodded. "Maybe."

"Hercaleon, make the arrangements." Geral leaned back on his cushions and crossed his arms.

"For the trade, or the agreement?" Hercaleon was fairly sure he knew what Geral was talking about but wanted clarification.

"The trade, boy, the trade." Geral huffed.

"Right." Hercaleon knew Abu was just outside, sitting on the shelf with Felmar. "Abu, can you escort our healer and bring her a few tusks from the storeroom to choose from, and a couple of the larger hides." He smiled at the healer as she started past. "Unfortunately, the skins aren't as large as they could be. The dragons are still learning to eat the meat while preserving the hides. They have also just begun to dry."

"I understand." She nodded. "I will return next week to see to Geral's bones." Without a look back toward the bed, she left the room.

"She's a friendly one." Hercaleon chuckled as he walked back to Geral. "Are you up for a few questions?" He felt a little bad for ambushing the trainer but wanted to know what was going on before he pushed the new flight harder than they were ready for.

"Sure." He glanced out his bedchamber. "Do you trust the old boy?"

"Abu?" Hercaleon didn't want to go into how well he'd begun trusting Abu in the days since the hunt. "Yes. He's a little old for a trainee, but not the eldest I've seen. He's got a good head on his shoulders, even if he is the one who banged you up."

"Did he tell you that, or one of the others?"

"I figured it out, and he feels sorry about it." Hercaleon shoved off the wall and started pacing near the bed. "He did the same to me, but we were up higher. Chromath threw him off his dragon, then saved me."

"Felmar wanted to do more than just throw him." It was Geral's turn to chuckle. "But yeah, he's a good man. Mostly likely going to be flight leader in a couple of months when we head back to Lestian."

"These trainees aren't ready to go back to Lestian. From what they've said, they've barely had a chance to fly cloud level or above."

Geral shrugged, then grimaced in pain. "So. Most of our fighting is below cloud level. They're ready."

"Why have you kept them below cloud level? When I was trained…by you…we were higher than this lot." Hercaleon stopped and stared at Geral laying in the bed. He looked a lot older than he had ten years earlier when Hercaleon had gone through training. Gone was the fire of a man determined to get the most out of his trainees, no matter the cost. There was a look, it wasn't constant, but Hercaleon had seen it a couple of times, that said Geral wished he'd died in the accident that left him broken.

"Azure Wing was tougher than these…than Lapis. You had some fighter training before you bonded with your dragons. There were more of you." Geral frowned and looked at his hands. "There were more of all of us."

"And if Lapis Wing isn't trained right, there will be fewer of them faster than there were fewer of any wing before them." Hercaleon started pacing again.

"Then toughen them up, Hercaleon. Toughen them up." Geral pounded the bed with his good hand. "If you think they aren't up to it, then make them. I'm not going to be a blue trainer forever. I'll see that the warlord knows your name if you can get this flight combat ready, so they don't all die within the first year. Now, get out of here and make sure that Bastette bitch doesn't take all the good stuff. We need to get some things back to Lestian for the war effort."

"I'll do my best." Hercaleon turned and strode out of the cave. He still didn't know why Geral hadn't been taking the trainees higher, but he had permission to do what he needed to. With Abu's help, he could get the flight ready for combat.

Hercaleon straightened in his saddle and looked out over the flight in a tight, three-tier, diamond formation. After two weeks of work, the flight was actually doing it right. It was impressive. Abu and Lukeom were in the lead point position. It wasn't a hard formation to fly, but it could be hard to hold if the opposition was coming in hot and heavy. Since he and Chromath were the only attackers, he didn't need to worry about that.

"Okay, let's do this. Through the middle of them. Let's see if they can hold it together." Hercaleon settled in the saddle and patted Chromath's neck.

"Right. Time to scatter them to the four winds." Chromath folded his wings in tight and cut through the sky like a blue arrow.

The formation was missing a central part—the large dragon, normally a brown, but occasionally a red, that the blue dragons were supposed to protect. But it left a perfect spot for Chromath to swing around, change direction, and generally cause havoc with the trainees.

Chromath dove through the formation, and nobody moved. He spun around and then dropped to the lower point dragon. Cutting it close enough he could've caused wing damage if he'd have wanted to, he nudged the dragon out of formation.

With a complaining roar, the displaced dragon got back into position.

Chromath chuckled. *"They're learning."*

"Then let's try something new." Hercaleon twisted and reached into his saddle bags for the smoke bombs he'd brought along.

Something creaked in his riding straps and his left leg was suddenly free. He wobbled and fell to the right.

"What are you doing?" Chromath snapped. *"Trying to fall off?"*

Hercaleon dropped the smoke bombs and grabbed his saddle, thankful Chromath hadn't been in the middle of a complex maneuver when that had happened. "Strap malfunction." He grabbed the strap and stared at what looked to be a cut near where the fixed end was sewn into the saddle. It was cut about halfway through. If he'd been less of a rider, he'd have lost his balance and fallen. Had they been lower, the fall could've been fatal.

"On my saddle?" Chromath growled. *"That's it. No more nice dragon."* He flapped his wings, forcing Hercaleon hard into the saddle.

"What are you doing?" Hercaleon dropped the strap, letting it dangle and bang against Chromath's scaly hide. He grabbed the front of the saddle and hung on.

"Nobody tries to hurt my rider." Chromath took a deep breath and let out a stream of fire as he approached one of the younger dragons.

The dragon rolled as its rider shouted and clung to the saddle.

"Chromath, we can't hurt them. We need them." Hercaleon pounded on Chromath's neck to get his attention.

"I'm trying to find out who's cutting the damned straps." He spun around and flamed the dragon, who folded his wings just in time and dropped below Chromath's attack.

Hercaleon stopped pounding on Chromath and stared as the formation fell apart, the young dragons flying away from Chromath. The older blue dragon had missed two attacks on the younger ones.

"You're not trying to hurt them."

"No. I have more control of my flames than that." Chromath came around again. *"I'm getting answers."*

"It would help if you weren't scaring me." Hercaleon smiled. Sometimes dragons could get one step ahead of their riders. Chromath always kept him on his toes.

"Lukeom's in position. Get ready."

"For what?" Hercaleon's heart pounded harder.

"Let go and fall." Chromath pumped his wings and shot straight up into the blue sky.

After twelve years of being bonded, he did what his dragon suggested, although it was counter to everything he'd trained himself to do. Hercaleon let go. His right foot caught on the intact strap, and he got yanked until he pointed his toe so it slipped out. Then he was falling. As soon as he was clear of Chromath, he spread his arms and legs and looked around for Lukeom and Abu.

Lukeom's head appeared right below him. Then the dragon's neck.

When Hercaleon was level with the leading edge of Lukeom's wing, he held both arms down.

"Got you." Abu's strong hands closed around his.

They both jerked backward, but Abu's riding straps held. He shifted slightly in the saddle so Hercaleon could swing his legs around and get settled behind him. It wasn't overly comfortable, but he was in a saddle on dragonback.

Above them, Chromath was roaring and spouting flames, acting like he was completely freaking out. Lapis Flight was scattering at his attack.

"Go land." Chromath ordered.

"You okay?" Abu twisted slightly as Hercaleon wrapped his arms around his chest.

Not able to help himself, Hercaleon kissed the side of his face. "Yes. Thanks for being there to catch me."

"Let's not do this again, okay?" Abu leaned into his embrace. "I'm just finding you. I don't want to lose you."

Lukeom had angled toward the ground and was flying in a slow, lazy circle, that was more of a glide than a flight. Standard pattern for a dragon on a rescue flight.

"You're not going to lose me." Hercaleon hugged Abu tightly. He wasn't the first man, or even first dragon rider, Hercaleon had been with, but he was the first that Hercaleon had thought about keeping. "Now, let's hope Chromath gets some information out of the rest of the flight."

There was a scream above them.

A rider was falling, flailing his arms and legs.

"Chromath, if his dragon doesn't catch him, you have to." Hercaleon wished he was in the saddle at that point.

An irritated huff came from his dragon.

"Can we do anything?" Abu looked down as the rider disappeared into the clouds.

"Lukeom's not big enough to carry three." Hercaleon pointed off to the side as Chromath followed the rider into the clouds. "Chromath'll catch him." He glanced up at the disarray of dragons and riders above them. "Lukeom, tell everyone to land at the river."

Abu nodded. "Done."

The clouds closed around them, cutting off his view from either above or below.

Hercaleon kissed the back of Abu's neck. "I've never flown with a guy I liked before."

Abu chuckled. "I can't say as I have either. You're the first since I bonded."

They cleared the clouds as the flight was starting to land below them.

Chromath had a rider in his talons, not on his back. *"I got him."*

"You caught him, or he's the one who's been cutting straps?"

"Both. I should've let him hit the ground." Chromath folded his wings again and dropped through the flight that was slowly descending. A scream came from the rider.

"Isn't he being a little rough?" Abu muttered.

"That's the one who's been cutting straps. He put me in danger. If I hadn't told Chromath to catch him, he'd have let him splat." Even so, Hercaleon wasn't totally sure what they were going to do with him. It was against the law to harm either a dragon or a rider. If dragons decided to take justice into their own talons, Chromath could eat him.

In Hercaleon's embrace, Abu shuddered. "Dragons letting riders die is against the rules, isn't it?"

"*Isn't* it?" Hercaleon repeated Abu's words incredulously. "Hasn't Geral taught you all the basic rules of being a dragon rider?"

"We follow orders, and attack Sielew. That's about it."

"No." Hercaleon shook his head. "That's not about it. Dragons are sacred. You don't do anything that would injure a dragon. If dragons injure one another, that's one thing, but riders don't hurt dragons. We also don't hurt each other. It's strictly forbidden. Again, dragons can hurt us, but we can't hurt each other." They were things new riders of Hercaleon's time had learned in the first days after reaching the Valley of the Mists. Why hadn't Geral told this group of riders?

Lukeom landed gently amongst the other dragons.

Chromath landed in front of him, keeping the guilty rider in his grasp, suspended just a few feet off the ground.

The rider's dragon roared several times as he swooped in on Chromath like an angry crow trying to drive off a hawk.

"Stop that!" Hercaleon shouted at the offending dragon as he jumped off Lukeom's back. It was a lot easier than jumping from Chromath.

Stomping past the confused riders and dragons as riders dismounted, Hercaleon walked up to Chromath. "Put him down."

"I should just eat him." Chromath shook the rider again, and then lowered him to the ground.

"If these riders had been taught what they should've, I'd let you." Hercaleon grabbed the rider by the collar. *"But they weren't."* He was fairly sure which rider he was dealing with, but he yanked off the trainee's helmet and goggles, just to make sure. "Tym."

Tym's dragon, Nyke, landed and stomped toward them until Chromath flared his wings and growled.

Squirming, Tym refused to meet his gaze. "What?"

"You've tried to kill me and Abu. What do you have to say for yourself?" Hercaleon glared at him.

"Abu tried to kill Geral." Tym's voice was barely a whisper, as he continued to stare at the ground.

"No, he didn't. That was a really bad accident." Hercaleon yanked up Tym by the belt and carried him like a saddle to Geral's cave.

Geral was propped up in bed reading. "What's going on?"

Hercaleon finally set Tym down; even with his dragon-enhanced strength, the effort of carrying a man with one hand all the way from the valley floor was a bit draining. "This rider has been cutting the riding straps of other riders. Abu, and myself."

"Tym." Geral set his book down. "Is this true?"

Shuffling his feet, Tym finally looked up, but to stare at Geral, not Hercaleon. "Abu tried to kill you, when he knocked you off Felmar. You haven't been able to defend yourself, so I had to."

Geral swung his feet over the side of the bed and looked like he was going to try to stand but stopped himself. "Boy, if Abu had meant to kill me, rest assured Felmar would've killed him and his dragon for that."

A chill went through Hercaleon at the idea of Felmar eating Abu and killing Lukeom. It was the dragon rider way, but he didn't want to see them meet such a fate.

"I didn't know that." Tym turned from Geral and looked at Hercaleon. "Honestly, I didn't. I thought since Geral was injured, someone else needed to defend him." He looked back at Geral. "Sir. You've been so good to me. I had to try to make things right."

With a heavy sigh, Geral pointed to the bedchamber door. "Go to your cave. Take your dragon too. You're grounded until I figure out what needs to be done. If you step out of your cave, or Nyke leaves his shelf, I will let Chromath and Lukeom deal out dragon justice to both of you."

Tym started to shake. "Yes, sir." He turned and ran from the cave, tears streaming down his face. Seconds later Felmar roared and then there were more footsteps hurrying down the path from the cave.

Geral pinched his nose and closed his eyes before laying back on his pillows. "What do we do with that one?"

Hercaleon took the opening. "Before we get to that, I have some more questions for you."

"Sure." Geral sighed. "What do you need to know?"

Doing his best to keep his own temper, Hercaleon laid out the questions about the lack of training, right down to basic rider etiquette. There was so much.

When he was done, Geral just frowned, then shook his head. "Boy, have you ever felt like you outlived your usefulness?"

It wasn't the response Hercaleon had expected. "I can't say as I have." Some of the anger he'd felt at Geral evaporated.

"Well, if you live as long as I have, then you might eventually start feeling that way. I don't know how Warlord Tygar keeps going. For almost twenty years, I've been the last member of Sapphire Flight. That's one of the reasons I got assigned as blue dragon trainer. Other than Queen Aquanius's rider Celestia, I'm the oldest blue dragon rider. Since the war began, we've forgotten how long we can really live, because we blue riders die so quickly."

Hercaleon stayed quiet, thinking how few members of Azure Flight there were. The larger dragons lived longer than the smaller ones, but he'd never stopped to think about how long he might really live. Was this one of the reasons riders were forbidden to have contact with non-riders, beyond the servants of Dragon Hill?

Again, Geral sighed. "I think I'm beyond my point of usefulness. I keep forgetting things, and the idea of flying too high is terrifying. I've done my best with this group, but I've been worried for a time that I was missing things. Maybe it's a good thing you came here. The accident has a silver lining."

"Why haven't you asked for help before now?" Hercaleon started pacing, trying to sort out everything he was hearing.

"I was afraid what would happen if I admitted my failings to Warlord Tygar. He isn't known for being understanding of weakness."

There was no way Hercaleon could deny that. "Do you have any ideas of what you want to do from here?"

"It might be nice to just get on Felmar and fly south until he can't fly no more. Maybe we could both fall in the ocean and meet a quiet end. After years of fighting, ending it quietly has an appeal."

Hercaleon didn't want to talk about how his old teacher wanted to end his life, although it might give Geral some peace. "While you think about that, what should I do with Tym?"

Geral shook his head and closed his eyes. "Teach him. Teach them all. Do what I should've done over a year ago, when their dragons were still growing, and I was making sure they could fight. Hercaleon, I need you to do that for them. Fix my mistakes. And maybe, just maybe it's not too late to help them survive." He sank in on himself, looking more like a frail commoner than a strong dragon rider.

"I can do that." Hercaleon stopped pacing. "I'll send a message back to Dragon Hill that this hatching is going to be a few months late coming home." There wasn't another batch of eggs waiting to hatch, so they had time.

"Good." Geral slid down in the bed and pulled a blanket over himself.

Although Hercaleon wasn't sure things were settled, he had enough to get started. Without bothering Geral, he turned and walked out of the bedchamber.

On the shelf, he paused and looked at Felmar. The dragon's scales were tinged in gray, something he hadn't noticed before. He was looking into the cave where his rider lay, and looked as tired as Geral did. Maybe there was a point when dragons and riders just got old enough that their time was done.

"You're both ready for a rest." Hercaleon sighed as Felmar didn't even lift his head to look in his direction.

"Chromath. Tell Nyke that he is to stay on his shelf until morning. I'll be by then to talk with Tym."

"I'll do that. I don't think you and I are going to get old. I hope not."

"I don't know, my bond. I don't know." Hercaleon headed to the valley floor and his cave. It was going to be more than a temporary spot for him.

Inside the blacksmith's cave, Abu was sitting on a stool next to a workbench as Hercaleon walked in. "So, what's going to happen to Tym?"

With a couple of long strides, Hercaleon cleared the distance between them, and picked up Abu in a tight embrace. For several minutes he just stood there, holding him. He'd never felt like he had someone to come home to before. It was good to have someone to cling to, to help anchor himself in the world on a level even his bond with Chromath didn't.

After what seemed like an eternity, he let go of Abu and moved back just a little, then claimed his hand. "You know we probably won't live long lives, right?"

"Blue dragon riders aren't known for their longevity." Abu traced Hercaleon's jawline, leaving shivers in his wake. "That's why we love hard and fast."

"Like we live." At least Geral had told them that much. "I have to teach you lot to survive. But that really starts tomorrow."

Abu kissed him. "And tonight, you're mine."

"Yes." Hercaleon kissed him back.

When they parted again, he noticed Chromath's saddle and other gear hanging on the hooks and blocks they belonged on. "Did you untack Chromath?"

"Yeah." Abu nodded and nuzzled his neck. "Lukeom acted as an interpreter for us. I thought it might help you out."

It was very rare for a dragon to allow another rider to handle their tack. Chromath must be accepting Abu as part of their lives.

"And the dragons weren't on the shelf." Hercaleon felt a satisfied feeling coming from Chromath. He was eating down by the river, with Lukeom at his side. The two of them were also bonding. "Thank you for taking care of that."

"I took care of Lukeom first."

"Always. A rider always takes care of their dragon first." Hercaleon took Abu's hand and led him toward the bedchamber.

"And after that, we take care of our men and ourselves." Abu jumped on Hercaleon's back and kissed his head as he started undoing the straps that held Hercaleon's leather flight jacket closed.

"Exactly." Hercaleon surrendered himself to Abu. There would be time to deal with everything else. In that moment, it just felt nice to have someone want him and want to make him feel good.

There was a brief sound of dragon wings as Chromath and Lukeom landed on the patio in front of the forge, then Hercaleon wasn't aware of anything beyond Abu helping alleviate the stresses of the day.

From the Author

Where did the inspiration for *Falling* come from? Well, that's a two-fold answer. A few months ago, one of my co-authors was playing around with an AI art program and it coughed up some really interesting pictures of people and dragons. Several things came together at the same time. Things like what makes a great fantasy novel, the Israel Hamas War, me being in a dark place, and the AI dragon and rider pictures. My brain took all that input, threw it in my cranial blender and the first bits of my Bloody Skies series poured out.

In that series, the character of Hercaleon, with his dragon, Chromath plays a fairly pivotal role. When I spotted the open call for a first meeting LGBTQ+ romantic short story, the blender started up again and after a few days of churning, as I finished the first draft of book one, I was putting together how I wanted the story to go. Hercaleon needed a boyfriend. The story needed to be set about the time he became the blue dragon flight trainer. Thus was *Falling* taking shape. It didn't end up being exactly the way I planned it. I was thrilled when Sam said we didn't have to do a HEA, or even a HFN ending, although that's what I ended up writing. Hercaleon and Abu wanted to end up happy. In a time of war and darkness, we all need as much happiness as we can get, so *Falling* ends happy...for now.

About the Author

A.M. has been writing to pass the time since high school. The stories he wrote helped him deal with life. A few years ago, he started sharing those stories with friends who enjoyed them, and he has started sending his works out into the world to share with other people. He lives in the mountains with his extremely supportive husband. They have a lot of critters, including dogs, cats, birds, horses, and rabbits. When not writing, A.M. spends a lot of time hiking, trail riding, or just driving in the mountains. Nature provides a lot of inspiration for his work and keeps him writing. He is also an avid photographer and falconer. Don't get him started talking about his birds, because he won't stop for a while.

Web Contact Info:
Website: www.amburns.com
Email: andy@amburns.com
Facebook: www.facebook.com/authoramburns

To Say Sorry

by
Rob Nisbet

To Say Sorry

J ane stormed out of the house and jabbed at the door release on her car key. The car beeped and flashed its lights as Jane yanked open the door and flung herself heavily onto the driver's seat.

"An affair?" Jane seethed to herself. Chris was so suspicious; where would she find the time for an affair? Yes, she regularly met people at work, men included, but that was her job. An events organiser *had* to meet people. And Chris thought that these men would be after her because that's what men were like.

"Men!" she cried aiming the word at the front door of her neat townhouse. She sat in the car and allowed herself a full couple of minutes to calm down before driving. Really, Chris was intolerable. So many questions: who would she be meeting today? Were these people married? Exactly what time would she be back? And if she were even a few minutes late there would be a barrage of further questions. Where had she been? Who had she been with? And Chris wouldn't believe her, no matter what she said. And then would come the accusations, and she knew that she couldn't cope with that anymore.

Jane drove to the station car park still in a fog of fury. She jumped a red light and blared her horn at the other motorists who dared get in her way. The argument had made her late and now she sped between the rows of cars, anxious that she wouldn't find a space. There ahead, on the bend at the furthest point of the car park, was the last space. Jane sent up a prayer of thanks to the God of parking spaces and pulled in, only to screech to a halt.

Another car from the other side of the bend had had the same idea and with a scrape of rubber the two cars stopped, their bumpers only inches apart.

Jane instantly thumbed the window switch ready to shout at the other driver. In her way was a gleaming yellow sports car, low to the ground, and with the top down. A young man strained against his seat belt to see how close the cars were. He ran a hand through his sleek mane of blond hair and held up a hand in chivalrous apology.

The yellow car pulled back and Jane swiftly claimed the parking space. She was about to raise the window when she saw that the young man was outside looking in at her. Just a boy, thought Jane. She guessed he must be about five years younger than her: mid-twenties at the most.

"Are you okay?" he asked, looking anxious. "That was pretty close."

Jane twisted out of the door and, with a beep, locked it behind her.

"I'm perfectly fine," she said, looking past this stranger; if she were quick, she might still catch the half-past. But the young man was standing in front of her and seemed to be waiting for more of a response. "Look," she said, annoyed. "I've had a bad morning. I'm stressed, I'm late, and you're in my way."

The man grinned with perfect white teeth. "I thought you might have been a bit shaken—Jane."

Jane looked curiously into his blue eyes, his tanned face, his open-necked shirt. "Do I know you...?" Then she remembered the badge she wore. As well as the company logo it had her name: Jane Prince – Events Organiser.

"Is Prince your maiden name?" he asked.

The question took Jane by surprise. "Yes," she said before she could stop herself, "it is."

"I'd like to say sorry properly," said the young man waving casually at his sleek yellow car. "You know—for the near accident. I thought perhaps, dinner?"

For a few seconds Jane couldn't think what to say. Chris was right after all about men, they *were* all the same.

Jane managed a smile of surprised amusement then squeezed past the man before he took the smile as one of encouragement. "Dinner?" Jane threw the idea back at him scornfully. She glanced at his clothes, his hair, his car: all too flashy, too confident. Contrived, no doubt, to wow the entire female species.

Well not this time. Jane shook her head, "You're definitely not my type," she said and, turning, dashed for her train.

That evening Jane got back to the station exactly on time. At least Chris wouldn't be able to moan about her getting home late tonight.

As Jane walked to her car at the far end of the car park, she noticed, on the bonnet, a splash of yellow. She picked up her speed, and there, held in place by one of the windscreen wipers, was a bunch of yellow roses. Jane stood by the car and looked around, but the few people in sight seemed completely uninterested in her or the flowers.

Jane pulled the flowers free; they were gorgeous and obviously expensive. She got into the car, then she saw the card. It was a little florist's label with one word scrawled across it: "Sorry."

No name, but then, Jane realised, she didn't know his name. She tossed the roses onto the passenger seat. Yes, they were beautiful, but how flashy and how presumptuous. And how dare he just leave flowers on her car like that. Suppose Chris had seen them.

Oh God, what a nightmare that would have been.

Jane drove out onto the high street with the velveteen scent of roses filling the car. What on Earth should she tell Chris? Not the truth certainly. She would never hear the end of it. And their relationship was strained enough just at the moment.

As she drove home, Jane pictured Chris and the unnamed young man, as if in a vision, side by side. Chris in a shapeless jumper, the young man in a sharply tailored suit and with a yellow rose in his buttonhole for good measure. Apart from the very obvious physical differences, Jane realised that the young man stood for everything she loathed. She'd hardly met him, but her mind conjured-up a loud conceited show-off, full of his imagined self-importance, thinking he could pull some stranger in the car park with a bunch of flowers. In short, he was what Chris would call a 'typical man.'

Jane drove into her street. She had decided that perhaps it would be best to say nothing of the flowers, just leave them in the car and dispose of them later. She should have left them behind at the station, but that seemed such a waste, and anyway it was too late for that now. Jane pulled-up outside the neat little townhouse and couldn't believe her eyes. There, parked just a few yards away, was the unmistakeable yellow sports car. Jane blinked as if to banish some illusion, but the car remained, stubbornly conspicuous.

Without pausing to think, Jane leapt out of her car and looked around. Instantly the young man stepped out from behind her neighbour's hedge.

"Hello, Jane Prince," he said smiling.

"What…?" Such impudence! Jane was momentarily tongue-tied.

The man gestured to Jane's badge. "I recognised the logo," he said, "then phoned your company. I explained to someone there about our encounter this morning and that there was a romantic dinner at stake. They were very helpful, but then I *was* very persuasive."

Jane resolved to have more than a few stern words with whoever had given out her home address. "You cheeky…" Jane clenched her fists then realised that she was holding the bunch of yellow roses. Well, now seemed the perfect time to return them.

"You're so sure of yourself, aren't you?" she said, then whacked him around the head with the flowers.

The young man staggered back with such an astonished look of surprise on his tanned face that it was almost comical.

Behind Jane the door of the town house was pulled open; Chris had been watching for her arrival and had come out to see what was going on.

Jane continued her attack. "Are you so arrogant," she cried, "that you can't understand the word *no*?" She hit him again in a hail of yellow petals. "I said you're not my type. Can't you see I'm not remotely interested?"

Jane swept back the roses to strike again then she felt Chris touch her on the arm. "Hey," said Chris. "Careful. Those flowers cost me a fortune."

"You?" It was Jane's turn to be surprised.

Chris nodded. "When you stormed out this morning, I—well, I realised that I'd been giving you such a hard time lately. The roses were a surprise, to say sorry."

Jane's fury melted instantly, and she turned quite calmly to the battered young man. "Prince *is* my maiden name," she said. "I'm not married, but I *do* have a partner." Jane put her arm around the woman that had appeared from the house. "This is Christine. *Now* will you believe I'm not interested?"

From the Author

I have read several stories, some by established authors, where I felt the 'narrator' in the tale had lied to the reader.

One, for example, concerned a pig, which was referred to as 'he' throughout the story—until the surprise twist ending where she is revealed to be pregnant!

I felt the author had deceived the reader. So...I wanted to try a similar story but playing fair, so that, even on a second reading, the reader would see that the narrator had been strictly truthful.

Agatha Christie was adept at this 'truthful deception,' sometimes using phrases which could be taken two ways, leading the reader to *assume* something that was actually false.

I don't claim to be an Agatha Christie, but I am happy that "To Say Sorry" may mislead the reader but not actually lie to them.

About the Author

Rob Nisbet lives in a small clifftop town on the English south coast near Brighton. He has had over 100 stories printed in anthologies and magazines ranging from romance (using his wife's name) to horror. His wife has recently turned to crime.

He started writing as a hobby, prompted by an evening class with his first sale to *Woman's Weekly*. Many 'womag' sales followed.

With an interest in speculative fiction, he branched into horror including five volumes in the Castle of Horror series. Sci-fi credits include audio drama. He has adapted work by Philip K. Dick for radio and, to date, has had seven audio scripts produced by Big Finish/BBC for their Doctor Who range.

He has won five international writing competitions with prizes ranging from a mug & t-shirt to a Mediterranean cruise. He was also the winner of the 2022 Kepler Award for a sci-fi/fantasy short story.

The Last Gift of Blockbuster

by
Kay Hanifen

The Last Gift of
Blockbuster

My alarm went off at exactly midnight, but I had been too excited to sleep, so I just shut it off, grabbed the shoebox from the corner of my closet, and, sneaking past Lizzie's room, crept downstairs. My cell phone buzzed, and I slid it open. It's a little embarrassing to have a phone that you have to slide open when all your friends have the new iPhone 4, but Mom and Dad say I'm gonna have to wait until my birthday in June to get one.

"We don't want you meeting any strange men from the internet," they would always tell me, as if I wanted to talk to men. Or even boys, really. Middle school boys were stupid. I just didn't get what other girls in my grade saw in them. They all had braces or acne or smelled bad.

The text from Chelsea announced that she was here waiting outside the front door, so I opened it and let my best friend in from the cold. Mom and Dad were away for the night at some weekend couples' retreat, so I was alone with my little sister, Lizzie. They said not to open the door for anyone but the neighbor who was supposed to check in on us. But, after school today, I'd biked to the Blockbuster. I don't know why they're going out of business. I love going there. It has this distinct smell like plastic, vinyl, and overly air-conditioned office building, and I love wandering the rows of movies until I find something I missed in theaters or a hidden gem that, a few years from now, I will remember like a fever dream. The texture of the DVD cases is different there too. I like running my fingernails up and down and feeling the subtle vertical ridges running the length of the plastic.

Whenever we went as a family, Mom and Dad had one rule: no scary movies. They didn't like horror movies, and didn't want me to have nightmares, or worse, for Lizzie to watch with me and have nightmares. I didn't know why. Scary movies were cool! I would always wander up and down the aisles staring at the creepy DVD covers and reading the synopses because Mom and Dad couldn't stop me from doing that even if they complained I was taking too long.

Obviously, when I went on my own to the liquidation sale, I made a beeline for the scary movie aisle and picked up all the classics that hadn't already been bought out—*Friday the 13th Part VII: Jason Takes Manhattan, Jason X, Nightmare on Elm Street 2,* and *Child's Play*—along with some newer stuff like *The Devil Inside, Lake Placid, The Hills Have Eyes,* and *Amusement.* It emptied out my allowance and all the babysitting money I'd saved, and I didn't know much about these movies, but I was excited to watch them with Chelsea.

We'd been close ever since she moved in, because she was the coolest person I've ever met. She died her blonde hair bright blue, dressed all in black, and had a black belt in Taekwondo, which freaked out Mom, Dad, and Lizzie at first, but then, when they got to know her, they realized, like I had, that she was super sweet. She used her tough looks to scare bullies away from the younger grades and the special needs kids, and she always helped me with my math homework.

When she stepped through my front door for our secret scary movie night, she looked me up and down with a smirk and said, "Nice PJs. Ninja Turtles are cool." She gestured to her blue hair. "Guess which one's my favorite."

My face colored as I looked down at the green shirt and pants patterned with the classic eighties' turtles. I liked the one they showed on Saturday mornings on 4Kids, but the new Nickelodeon version was also pretty good. I should've put something else on, but these were my favorite, and I wanted to feel comfortable tonight. "Uh, thanks. He's mine too."

Glancing around the foyer, she asked, "Are you sure your parents aren't coming home tonight?"

"One hundred percent." I grinned and pulled her into the living room where I had set the shoebox and turned on the TV. Our massive dinosaur of a television still worked, so we hadn't switched to a flatscreen just yet. A late-night comedian was making jokes about something I didn't get—probably the election or the Mayan Calendar ending the world before climate change got us. "Go ahead and pick something out," I said as I shoved a packet of popcorn into the microwave and set the timer for two minutes.

She grinned and held up the box with the scary nun on the front. "Devil Inside?"

Exorcism stories always freaked me out, so I was kinda hoping to build up to it, but I also didn't want to look like a chicken in front of Chelsea. "Sure." The popcorn began popping, making me jump.

She laughed. "It hasn't even started yet."

The movie wasn't really scary. The camera was too shaky, and the plot didn't make much sense. The ending, though, made us both mad. The main characters all got into a car crash and then there's a link to a website? That's it?

"What the heck was that?" Chelsea cried as she threw up her hands. We were so mad we forgot that Lizzie was asleep upstairs, and that we needed to keep it down.

"Laura?" Lizzie asked, yawning from the staircase.

"Shit," slipped out, and her eyes widened in shock.

"You swore." Her eyes danced from me to Chelsea to the shoebox of DVDs before settling on the end credits rolling with spooky music playing over it. Her lips curled into a wicked grin. We were caught, cornered like a big-boobed bimbo in a slasher movie. "I'm telling Mom and Dad."

I leapt to my feet and dragged her by the arm out of Chelsea's earshot. "Don't you dare."

"Then let me watch with you." Her eyes sparkled as though she believed she'd already won.

"Absolutely not. You'll have nightmares," I hissed.

"And you won't?"

"No, because I'm not ten."

"You're only three years older than me. And I promise I won't tell Mom you brought Chelsea here if I do have nightmares." She fixed me with her most effective puppy dog eyes, pouting with her lower lip out.

I couldn't exactly say no, so I just crossed my arms. In my history class, we learned all about the Cold War and the idea of mutually assured destruction. Basically, the only thing that kept us from blowing ourselves off the face of the planet was the understanding that once someone fired the nukes, then everyone was gonna do it, and the world will end. "Fine, but if you have to make your own popcorn and if you tell, I'll tell Mom that you were the one that tore her favorite dress because you decided to try it on during your playdate with Rosie last month."

She squealed in delight and threw her arms around my waist. "Thank you, thank you!"

Chelsea looked vaguely amused as we both returned to the living room, Lizzie looking triumphant and me clearly the loser. Lizzie threw another packet of popcorn into the microwave while Chelsea and I set out the DVDs to decide what to watch next.

Because Lizzie was terrified of clowns, I left *Amusement* in the box for later. I may have been annoyed with her, but I didn't want her to be traumatized. I wasn't a monster. Once again, the pops sounded through the house, and while she waited for her own bowl, she approached to peer over our shoulders.

As we debated whether to go with *A Nightmare on Elm Street 2* or *Lake Placid*, Lizzie piped up by asking, "What about *Face of Fear*?"

We both looked at her like she'd grown two heads. "We're just watching the DVDs I bought at Blockbuster," I said.

"You did, though," she said, and like a magician pulling a rabbit from her hat, she held up the plastic bag, branded with the Blockbuster logo, that I'd saved in the box because I thought that I might want another keepsake from the store. It very clearly held another DVD.

"What the hell?" I exclaimed, snatching the bag from her hands, and ignoring her cry of "Hey!" There was no way that had been in the box earlier. I knew exactly what I bought and this DVD, with the pale-yellow cover emblazoned with the store's logo and the movie's title, was not one of them.

"Maybe the store clerk decided to just give it to you?" Chelsea suggested, her expression looking as confused as I felt. "They're trying to get rid of as many movies as they can. Could he have slipped it inside while you were at the register or something?"

I shook my head. "No, I would definitely have noticed before now."

She giggled. "Maybe it's a cursed DVD like *The Ring*. We watch it and a ghost kills us in seven days." Her eyes had this mischievous glint to them, the kind of smile that meant that she was about to try something either very clever or very stupid. Usually, I liked that gleam in her eye, but I was too freaked out by the surprise DVD. "We should watch it," she said.

I gave her a flat look. I didn't care if she thought I was lame or stupid for not going along with this. Satan would be ice-skating to work before I agreed that it's a good idea. "Do you want to die like the dumbest character in a horror movie?" I asked.

"Are you scared?" Lizzie teased in that obnoxious singsong voice that all younger siblings are born knowing. But unlike our pact of mutually assured destruction, I had logic on my side.

"It's called having common sense. You should try it." I got to my feet and threw the DVD into the garbage can. It didn't matter if I looked scared in front of Chelsea. That movie gave me a terrible feeling in the pit of my stomach, and I wanted it as far away from me as humanly possible. "Let's do *Lake Placid*. I heard Betty White's in it."

Lizzie and Chelsea exchanged confused glances and then shrugged at each other. *Laura was acting weird and crazy. Must be a Tuesday.* Chelsea might never want to see me again after the weirdness tonight, but I wouldn't in a million years watch that movie. "Sounds good," Chelsea said, handing me the DVD case.

Unlike the typical DVD that started with the anti-pirating warning and then showed movie trailers before going into a menu screen, it started with the inside of a familiar living room. Two girls—one with blue hair and the other a light brown—sat on a couch snacking on popcorn while a third squatted in front of the DVD player. It was us.

"What the hell?" I whispered, falling back on my butt to watch my doppelganger onscreen do the same. Heart pounding, I ejected the DVD, and threw it away, but instead of seeing a message saying, "No Disk," all three of us were still on the screen.

"Laura, if this is some kind of prank, it's really weird," Chelsea said as she bit her lip, anxiously tearing away at skin.

"It's not a prank," Lizzie answered for me, her terrified, wide eyes glued to the screen.

I backed away from the TV, my eyes fixed on the strange symbols that faintly ran across the screen like an afterimage when staring at a bright light or a magic eye painting. "We—we should call Mom and Dad. We'll tell them…" Tell them what? I had a cursed DVD and now I thought our TV was haunted? They were gonna kill me.

"Are you afraid?" someone—or something—whispered in my ear.

I shrieked and whipped around. "Did you hear that?"

Chelsea screamed, followed by Lizzie, and we ran to each other, huddling against the onslaught of whispers. I've fantasized a lot about being a hero, that I'd rescue someone (usually Chelsea) from a fire or a mugger and impress her enough that she decided to be my friend forever. Everyone else would finally notice the chubby, weird girl and they'd all want to be my friends too. Chelsea, of course, would still be my best friend, but now they'd all see what she saw in me.

In the moment, though, I didn't feel very heroic as I clung to them.

Come on. Think. How do you fight a demon? Garlic? Silver bullets? Crucifixes?

Before I could go hunting for my Catholic grandma's rosary, a cold, impossibly strong grip yanked my feet out from under me. I fell, landing on my wrist with a sickening crack that made me shriek. But it wasn't done.

The entity dragged me by the feet, my pajamas riding up on me as I was yanked all the way to my room. The door slammed shut behind me as I lay curled and shaking on the floor. "Laura," came the strangely familiar voice of a boy—an older teenager, probably.

I shakily sat up, terrified by what I'd find when I flicked on the light switch. My wrist throbbed with every beat of my racing heart. The room filled with warm, yellow light, and from the closet emerged a pale looking Justin Bieber. My jaw dropped, and I couldn't help but laugh. Was this the best the cursed DVD had to offer? A popstar I hate because he's annoying, his music sucks, and I have no idea why girls think he's so cute?

"What's so funny?" he asked, looking like a kicked puppy.

"You really think I'd be scared of Justin Bieber?" I giggled.

"I don't want you to be afraid of me, my love."

My laughter skidded to an abrupt halt. "Your what?"

He smiled, revealing pointed vampire teeth. "I've come to turn you so that we can live forever as vampires. It's what you've always wanted."

"On what planet?" I asked, crawling to the door, and turning the knob as he approached.

"Well, what girl doesn't want to be young, beautiful, and my girlfriend?" He grinned at that, and I swear I saw a glare off his pearly whites and heard a *ding*. "Come on. Kiss me. You know you want to."

"Absolutely not," I exclaimed, finally getting the door open and staggering out the other side. Half running and half limping, I stumbled down the stairs. The Justin Bieber vampire was right behind me, walking at a leisurely pace. Sprinting into the office, I grabbed a pencil. It was close enough to a stake that it should work.

I found Chelsea in the living room. She was pinned to the ceiling, writhing as disembodied hands that reached out from the ceiling tore away at her hair and clothes, and dirty, blackened fingernails scraped across her exposed flesh, shouting awful things like *freak, slut, bitch*, and saying that no one really cared about her. They were just afraid of her because she was so weird. No one could ever love a broken freak like her.

I stood transfixed for so long that I forgot two very important things. First, Lizzie wasn't with her, which could only mean that she was in the basement. Second, Vampire Bieber was right behind me. His ice-cold arms wrapped around my waist as he spun me around.

"There you are, baby girl," he said, and it made my skin crawl. Tilting his head, he asked, "Doesn't this form please you? All teenage girls think Justin Bieber is hot." Seeing the look on my face, he morphed, turning into each member of One Direction. "Come on, you know you want to be with me. An eternity of wealth and youthful beauty with a hot guy."

I struggled against his grasp, but it was too tight, and it made my broken wrist hurt so badly that I wanted to cry. "Let me go."

"Why? Why don't you want me?" he asked, his face morphing quickly from teenage boy to teenage boy, none of them attractive to me.

"I-I don't want any of you. I don't like boys!" I blurted out, and then covered my mouth. I'd never said that out loud before. I didn't want to admit it, even to myself. Mom and Dad loved me a lot, but they could also be pretty traditional. They'd said before that a marriage should be between a man and a woman, and, for a while,

I'm embarrassed to say that I agreed. At least, I did back then. Now, after seeing gay people on the internet and realizing that being against their rights would be like hating Martin Luthor King and the Civil Rights Movement, I'd changed my mind.

He smirked, his facial features settling into Chelsea's. "Something like this then. You want me. Admit it. Admit that you're a filthy and perverted sinner and that you deserve to be kicked out by your parents."

"Shut up," I growled, taking the pencil and stabbing Biebpire through the heart.

Chelsea's face looked at me with a mix of shock and betrayal that looked so real I began to doubt if I really got him. And then her knees gave out from under her, and panicking, I helped lower her to the ground. "No, no, no, no, no," I muttered as I tried to staunch the red blooming on her chest. She smiled, cupping my cheek and smearing red across it before falling back, her eyes vacant and staring.

But then I heard a muffled cry from above. Chelsea—the real Chelsea—was still pinned to the ceiling, a hand stuffed down her throat. She was choking on it, her face turning blue as she sank into the ceiling and those insults grew louder and louder.

"Let her go," I shouted, grabbing the nearby ottoman to stand on and reaching out my good hand.

The hands coming from the ceiling tore at my wrist, but I kept reaching for her. I was still a little short, my fingertips brushing hers. "Come on Chelsea. Take my hand," I said, straining to reach her.

With a cry muffled by the invading hand in her throat, she yanked one of her own free. I grasped it and pulled, yanking her down from the ceiling. We fell in a tumbling heap. If my wrist wasn't broken before, it almost certainly was now.

Chelsea clung to me, sobbing, and I clung back, feeling hot and cold all over. "It's you. It's really you," I mumbled over and over.

"Don't let go," she mumbled back.

A piercing scream from below reminded me that we couldn't stay like this forever. Lizzie was in danger. The demon must've dragged her to the basement. "Come on," I said. "Lizzie's still out there. We have to go."

I helped her to her feet, and we clung to each other as we headed to the basement. In the distance, the tinny sound of a circus organ played.

Clowns.

Lizzie was terrified of clowns.

And if any of them laid a hand on my little sister, I would wipe the painted grins off their faces with my fists.

As we took our final step off the basement stairs, the unfinished walkout changed. We were in the middle of an arena, surrounded by a jeering crowd.

Chelsea clutched me closer and pointed up. Though the concrete floor stayed the same, the tent reached far higher than the house. "Look!"

Lizzie stood, with a stick in hand, at one end of a platform. It connected to another on the opposite side of the big top by a rope. Clowns flanked her, forcing her forward onto the rope while the crowd jeered, "Baby! Scaredy cat! Wimp!"

She took a breath, and with nowhere else to turn, she took her first wobbly step onto the rope. Though she was high up, I could see the tears on her face glittering in the lights of the big top.

"You can do it, Lizzie." I ran to the other platform and began my ascent with Chelsea close behind. It was hard climbing with just one hand, but I had to do it. Lizzie may be an annoying little sister, but she was *my* annoying little sister. I periodically shouted my encouragements as I climbed, ignoring the swooping feeling in my own stomach. I wasn't scared of heights, but I was not a fan of them either.

"Come on Lizzie! I believe in you!" I shouted above the din, and soon, Chelsea joined. We were two voices against the jeers of dozens, but Lizzie's eyes flicked down to me when she was about a quarter of the way across the rope. She looked confused, but then smiled when I yelled, "You're so brave! I'll be right there on the other side!"

When she was three quarters of the way across, Chelsea and I finally reached the top. My wrist throbbed enough to bring tears to my eyes, but I still reached out for my sister. But I wasn't the only one trying to grab her. On the opposite platform, a clown jumped onto the rope. His grotesque pale face split into a wide, blood red smile, revealing razor sharp teeth. Despite his comically oversized shoes, he ran across with ease, and with the vibrations and the distraction, Lizzie lost her balance.

My heart leapt into my throat as something more terrifying than being forced to admit that I like girls, or my best friend (crush?) being pinned to the ceiling with a massive hand reaching down her throat, happened. My little sister wavered, tipped, and almost fell.

"Lizzie," I cried. I could see everything that happened next. The fall, the scream, the dull and meaty thud of flesh against concrete, and the crowd jeering at her small, broken body. Without thinking, I stepped onto the rope, Chelsea providing extra balance by holding my uninjured hand on the platform and keeping me steady. "Take my hand."

And by some miracle, she did not fall, making the crowd boo. Instead, she stumbled the final few feet to me, and Chelsea pulled us both onto the platform. I bit back a scream as it jostled the broken wrist, but Lizzie was here, and we were safe. At least, until the clown on the other side of the rope could reach us. He was already halfway there, his tongue lolling and eyes bright with joyful malice. If he caught us, he would enjoy whatever he did to us.

"We have to go," I said, nudging them both to the ladder.

When I reached solid ground, the world shifted once again, and we were back in the basement. Everything looked normal. If it wasn't for Chelsea's ripped clothes, Lizzie's tearstained cheeks, or my throbbing wrist, I would have thought none of it had happened.

But I knew that just because it looked over, it didn't mean that it was. Horror movie monsters always demanded a direct confrontation, and we'd faced its challenge, but not the monster itself. It was the cursed DVD that started all this. If we destroyed it, maybe we could get rid of the entity for good.

Chelsea seemed to have the same line of thought, because she began leading us in the direction of the staircase. Neither she nor Lizzy let me go as we ascended to the main floor.

The TV was on and showing our front door. It opened, revealing Mom and Dad with a couple of suitcases. They called our names, but we didn't answer, so they ventured farther into the house. It showed Chelsea in the living room with me, and we were making out. Like with tongue.

Seeing it made my face turn into a tomato, and beside me, Chelsea's face seemed to be making the same transformation.

The camera panned down to where Lizzie was lying on the floor, her head separated from her body, blood pooling below her like angel wings. Mom and Dad screamed, and Chelsea and I separated, taking our knives, and attacking. Chelsea took Dad while I took Mom, the blood staining my already rust colored pajamas. My blade sank into Mom's chest, and then back out, and in again. Over and over. Everything was stained bright red.

Chelsea stabbed Dad's chest and sliced down vertically, like dissecting a frog in science class. With a grin, she pulled out his entrails and wrapped them around her neck like the world's most disgusting feather boa.

My gorge rose, and I ran into the bathroom to retch up the remains of my popcorn. Lizzie threw up in the sink and Chelsea took the trashcan. Wiping my mouth, I sat back. They sat next to me, the three of us clinging to each other like we were victims of a shipwreck holding onto a broken bit of wood in a stormy sea.

"What is this thing?" Chelsea asked the air.

"I dunno. Aren't you the witch?" Lizzie snapped.

Chelsea rolled her eyes. "Just because I'm goth..."

"Guys," I said, interrupting before it could become a fight. "I think we have to destroy the DVD or maybe even the TV to get rid of it."

"If it keeps showing stuff like that, I don't think I can do it," Lizzie said. "I know that makes me a baby, but—"

"But nothing. You're not a baby," I said. "I'm sorry if I made you feel weak. I'm scared too." I thought back to the monsters we all faced. The first thing they did when they attacked was separate us. They were weaker when we were together. "But we can't separate, okay? It's stronger when we're alone."

"Maybe we should clear the air," Chelsea suggested. "I think it feeds on our fears and insecurities. But the entity lies, so we need someone on the outside to remind us of the truth."

"I'll go first," I said. "Lizzie, you are so incredibly brave. I mean you just tightroped across an entire circus while surrounded by evil clowns." I turned to Chelsea. "And you are the coolest, kindest person I've ever met. I like that you look tough and goth, and I want to be just like you, because you always seem so secure in yourself. I love the way your nose crinkles when you laugh, and your patchy blue dyed hair, and the way you always seem to know when to talk and when to listen. You're just the most amazing person I've ever met." My voice trailed off as my face turned beet red again. "Sorry. I don't know what you heard when I was fighting Vampire Justin Bieber, and I don't want to make you uncomfortable, but—"

She surged forward, pressing a kiss to my lips. Our breath smelled rank, and it was nothing like the kind of first kiss I daydreamed about, but it was still exhilarating. My lips still tingled when we separated. "I like you too. In-in case you can't tell."

Lizzie's gaze ping ponged between us. "Laura, you're gay?"

"I-uh, I mean, I think so. I only just admitted to myself that I like girls, but I-I don't know if—" My stupid stammering was interrupted by the feeling of Lizzie's arms around me and squeezing tight.

"I love you. Nothing will ever change that," she said.

I patted her back with my good arm. "I love you too."

Pulling back, she grinned. "Let's go destroy a cursed DVD." We all got to our feet and stepped out of the small bathroom that reeked of vomit. Hooking arms, we made our way to the living room as a unit, like Dorothy, the Tinman, and the Scarecrow on the Yellow Brick Road. *Lions and tigers and bears, oh my.*

Vampire Justin Bieber waited for us in the living room, flanked by clowns. Blackened hands reached from the walls and ceiling, trying to pull us into their cruel words. Biebpire grinned, revealing sharp fangs. "Hey girl. Come back for more?"

"We're not afraid of you anymore," I said, "so go away."

He laughed. "Do you think you can get rid of your fears that easily?" He morphed into Mom, and cried in her voice, "We'll get you help, counseling, anything to get you back on the right track." And then he looked like Dad and growled. "Get out. I never want to see your disgusting, perverted face ever again."

"Mom and Dad would never say that," Lizzie shouted, and the words undid the knot in my chest. She was right. They were a little old fashioned, but they loved me too much to reject me for being gay. I gave her a grateful squeeze.

"That's the thing about fear," the Thing-That-Wasn't-Dad said. "It's irrational and ever changing. Even if you know the truth, your heart still pounds, your chest still burns, and like the hydra, once you get over one fear, two will take its place."

"Maybe so," Chelsea said, "but you only have power over us when we give it to you. And I say you have no power over us." She led us through him and the clowns like they were nothing but mist, went to the DVD player, and hit the eject button. It opened, and we all took the DVD, breaking it apart. And with it, the images shattered.

My wrist throbbed as I staggered back to the couch. Mom and Dad would be home in the afternoon, and we needed to clean up and create a convincing lie to cover up my broken wrist.

I had no idea where that DVD came from, if there was more, or if the demon was gone just because we broke it. But with Lizzie and Chelsea beside me, I knew I could face it a hundred times more.

From the Author

This story was largely inspired by my nostalgia for Blockbuster Video. It went out of business when I was about the same age as the protagonist, Laura, and while I was not so sneaky that I bought horror films behind my parents' backs (or snuck friends into the house for secret sleepovers/movie nights), we did buy a bunch of DVDs at its liquidation sale. Before it closed, though, I have strong memories of wandering the aisles of Blockbuster. I would invariably end up in the horror section, and stare fascinated at the DVD covers. These were a sort of forbidden fruit to me, something I both feared and felt drawn to. Several of the titles I listed in the story were films I vividly remember seeing on the shelves, just waiting for popcorn and movie nights. I never did end up renting from that section, but I still have fond memories of it.

The other inspiration for this story was the coming out aspect. My coming out was markedly different from Laura's, but the friendship that blurs the line between best friends and crushes is something that I've lived through. When you were a queer preteen/teen girl in the early 2010's, you likely were not entirely aware of your own queerness. If you're like me, you were probably told that being gay is a bad thing and were on the cusp of thinking for yourself enough to know that this is not true. You may have had no interest in the typical pre-teen girl pop-culture of boy bands and sexy vampire boyfriends, and you and your best friend may have a relationship more intense than most, but that didn't mean you were gay. Until you are, and you realize that it's okay, because no matter what happens, you are loved. And not even a circus of evil clowns and a Biebpire can get in the way of that.

About the Author

I was born on a Friday the 13th and once lived for three months in a haunted castle. So, obviously, I had to become a horror writer. My articles have appeared in *Ghoul's Magazine*, *Screen Rant*, *The Borgen Project*, and *Leatherneck* magazine; and my short stories have appeared in almost fifty anthologies, including *Strangely Funny VIII*, *Crunchy With Ketchup*, *Dark Shadows: The Gay Nineties*, *Wicked Newsletters*, *Fearful Fun*, *Death of a Bad Neighbor*, *Enchanted Entrapments*, *Diet Riot: A Fatterpunk Anthology*, *M is for Medical*, *Terror in the Trenches*, *Slice of Paradise*, *Vinyl Cuts*, *Sherlock Holmes and Watson's Medical Mysteries*, *Beware the Bugs*, *Rockets and Robots*, *Divergent Terror*, and *Devil's Rejects*.

When I'm not consuming pop culture with the voraciousness of a vampire at a 24-hour blood bank, you can usually find me with my two black cats or at kayhanifenauthor.wordpress.com.

All the Leaves in the Trees

by
David J. Vane

All the Leaves in the Trees

The first time Rebecca spoke to Gabriel was in a German class they were both taking at the university. It was one o'clock on the dot when Rebecca swept into the room (after going over a litany of every conceivable verb in the English language, "swept" was the only one Gabe found that fit her presence that morning).

Who...? was all Gabe had time to think before she sat in the empty seat next to him and carefully crossed her legs under the desktop. It was Gabe's first class of the semester, and he found himself admiring her presence from his own desk, trying to be surreptitious but probably failing. He was a junior, and he hadn't really dated since his first year as a college student.

All he knew was that he couldn't stop noticing her tall black boots (lace-ups; no convenient zippers on the sides) or the few inches of toned, smooth leg leading from those boots to the hem of her skirt. He was immediately distracted by her dark purple top and tattoos peeking out on her shoulders, which the top didn't completely cover.

He knew that there were few empty seats in the classroom, and one of them happened to be next to him, but still, he imagined that sitting next to him was an intentional move on her part. Maybe it was his Pixies T-shirt, which seemed to coincide with her own fashion sense? It was impossible to tell but tempting to believe.

The first words she said to him, right before the professor started class, were, "You know, German books are always so much longer than English ones because their words are so damn long."

"Yeah—yeah, that's true," he stuttered in reply, and then, cheeks burning at the ineloquence of his answer, he pretended to take copious notes about the syllabus as the professor began his lecture.

Fifty minutes later, as they packed up and prepared to leave, he took the opportunity to try again.

"What were you drawing during class?" he asked, being careful not to sound too invested: just a guy asking a girl what she'd been up to in class, he told himself, that's all.

She'd already thrown her bag over her shoulder, and she tapped the strap with one finger as she turned to him. "Just a cartoon hippo." She shrugged.

"A hippo? Like, a hippopotamus? I have to be honest, that's not what I was expecting."

"Probably not, but there's a reason for it. We're in German class, and the German word for hippopotamus is *Nilpferd*. Literally, the horse of the Nile. Once you notice something like that, it's hard to forget."

They left the room together and started down the hall, toward the stairs and the main doors of the building.

"No way," he breathed. "That's awesome. Can I see it?"

That earned him a coy smile. "Not today, but maybe later?" Without waiting for an answer, she extended her hand. "I'm Rebecca."

"Gabe," he said.

She smiled again, but he thought he noticed a hint of hesitation this time, like she'd just remembered something troubling. This smile didn't reach her eyes, which he noticed were the pale blue-gray of troubled skies.

"See you next class, Gabe," she said, and turned to leave.

It took another two weeks for Gabe to get up the courage to ask for Rebecca's number and another week after that for him to ask her out. They talked every time they met for class, worked together on a communication project, and even ran into each other at the Target downtown; each time, they danced around their growing comfort with one another, and then retreated.

He finally took the chance when she showed him her sketches.

She did it when they were talking in a student lounge in the library one Friday, the two of them sitting in oversized easy chairs and watching the rain fall through the window. The skies outside were the color of steel, and the first hint of fall was in the air. This unwelcome change in weather had corralled them both into the library, and suddenly, Rebecca was turning to him and asking him if he'd like to see her attempt at drawing a horse of the Nile.

Most of the sketches she showed him that day were in the margins of her notebooks and class handouts. If she had a sketchbook, it didn't appear to get much use—and, likewise, the snippets of poetry and creative writing he showed her in turn were also scribbled in his notes and on class handouts. He thought the similarity in their processes was both amusing and, somehow, unsurprising.

"Tell me the truth," Rebecca said eventually, and again he marveled at how her confidence seemed to come and go depending on the topic. Sometimes, she seemed inevitable, like some elemental force, certain of herself to a fault. At other moments, though, that confidence slipped, and he saw another side of the person underneath. Bizarrely, it reminded him of the time he'd seen his high school teacher at the grocery store and realized that she was an entire person, with her own life and needs outside of the classroom.

He raised his eyebrows. "About your drawings?" he asked, and she nodded. "I like them. I like the giant anime eyes on the realistic animals, and I like the mix of cute cartoon figures laughing about death traps." He tapped a one-panel scene for emphasis: a child holding a balloon, floating above the ground, the wind pushing child and balloon over a pit of spikes.

"I mean, come on, that's just badass." Then, immediately afterward: "But I do have one question."

"Oh no," she answered with a laugh. "What is it?"

He steeled himself to do what he'd wanted to for weeks. "Do you want to get dinner with me this weekend? Not at the dining hall, like a real dinner."

She leaned across the arm of her chair and rested her chin on her hand. "Like, what, a date?"

He couldn't interpret her tone, but he wouldn't turn back now. "Yeah, like a date."

She grinned. "That would be really nice. But, if one date turns into more, there are some things I'd really want to tell you about me."

He smiled in return. "I'd love to listen."

That Saturday, Gabe picked up Rebecca and drove them to the only decent Thai restaurant in town. Downtown was always busy on the weekends: the bars packed with students; the cheap restaurants filled with pre- and, later, post-party crowds; and the nicer restaurants catering to anyone who was looking for a quieter atmosphere.

While they waited for their entrees, Rebecca peered at him over her drink and pointed a friendly finger in his direction. "Tell me about your family," she prompted. "I want to get to know you better."

Gabe thought for a moment before replying. "There's probably nothing exciting there. My parents split up when I was a kid and they're both remarried now. I live with my mom, and I have a brother, Sam. He's a senior in high school right now, and he's already told me he's not coming here for college. I think he wants to do his own thing—without his big brother watching over him."

"Mm-hmm. What else?" She carefully set her drink down on the table and turned to look at him more fully.

"I have a stepbrother who's my dad's kid in his new family. He's seven now, and I see them usually a few times a year. I'm not really as close to that part of my family, though. I think my dad is too preoccupied with his new life to worry too much about me or my brother. I know how that sounds, but I'm not bitter or anything."

"So, you get along with your mom?"

"Yeah, for the most part. She's pretty easygoing, and I've never been arrested or expelled, so she doesn't worry too much anymore. At least, not in an overbearing way. So, what about you?"

She shrugged. "I have an…uneasy relationship with my parents."

He waited, but she didn't say anything else.

"How so?" he ventured when it became apparent that she wasn't going to say more.

"They just don't really understand me. Like, they have a specific idea of who I should be, and this isn't it." To demonstrate, she gestured toward her black jeans and her boots. "They don't like my aesthetic, or…my identity. It's complicated."

"What, they don't like the punk rock/artist look? Because I think it's great."

"No, it's more than that—it's my whole philosophy of who I am. They just want different things for me."

"What do they want for you instead?"

Another pause followed, and then: "That's part of what I said I'd want you to know, if we started spending more time together. You know…more dates. But it's complicated, and I think I trust you enough to tell you this stuff, but I don't want to complicate things tonight. So, instead, I want to talk about why you chose German?"

The conversation flowed more easily from there. He'd started learning German in high school, mostly because his friends had also signed up for it, and then stuck with it when he found that he could pick it up easily. Rebecca had transferred the year before from a community college, which explained why they'd never seen each other in a German class before. They both liked nineties alternative and grunge music, and Rebecca was surprisingly knowledgeable about hip-hop and rap from that same era.

After dinner, Gabe dropped her back at her apartment and they parted with an awkward hug and a promise to make plans after class sometime in the coming week. She didn't invite him in, and he didn't ask.

He winced inwardly as he started his car and watched her disappear into her apartment. She lived off campus, in an old brownstone that had been converted into student apartments. Judging by the exterior alone, his own place was shabby compared to hers.

He lived alone in a tiny efficiency a few blocks away, but it could barely be considered livable. His building was all but crumbling, and he overloaded the breaker every time he ran the window air conditioner and the microwave at the same time. Apart from not having any roommates, the only upside was that it was ridiculously affordable because of its state of disrepair. He'd made it as comfortable as possible, but when you have to break the rules of the lease to bring in a space heater in the winter because the radiator didn't work, there was only so much you could do to improve the place. He wondered what she would make of it and hoped he wouldn't be embarrassed to show it to her if things came to that point.

As it turned out, Gabe didn't have to wait long to find out what Rebecca thought of his place. A few nights after their date, on Tuesday, Rebecca texted him sometime after midnight: WHAT'S THE GERMAN WORD FOR ROMANCE?

He guessed from her use of all caps that she was well on her way to being drunk, but he checked his German dictionary and texted her the answer (*das Liebeserlebnis*—literally, the experience of love), along with a plaintive request to come and keep him company instead of continuing to drink. As curiosity and worry gnawed at him, it struck him that he much preferred the lunches they'd shared under the huge tree on North Campus to this out-of-the-blue drunk text. He wondered distantly if this could be a sign of some new emotional maturity.

Another hour passed before she called him, the ring tone jarring him out of a dead sleep, and when he picked up, Rebecca was already midway into a sentence.

"…side on the street," she was saying. "I'm really, really, *really* (she dragged out the word with such vigor he could almost see the italics hanging in the air) sorry, but come let me in? It's pouring out here."

"I'll be right down," he told her, already pulling on his shoes. He stumbled down the narrow, paint-peeling hallway that led to the stairs and the street and held the door for her as she staggered into the building. She was shivering without her coat.

Upstairs, by the dim light of a single lamp, he saw that the bottoms of her jeans were soaked through a full foot up from the hem. She'd clearly walked through some puddles on her way over. He left her with a bottle of water and went to grab a towel from the bathroom to help her dry her hair. Returning a moment later, he found her slouching all the way down in his uncomfortable desk chair, halfheartedly pushing her boots against one another to get them off her feet.

"Here, let me," he murmured, and knelt before her to untie the laces and pull them off her feet.

"They stink," she giggled, and he wasn't sure if she meant the boots or her feet, but she let him pull off her socks and replace them with a dry pair of his own.

Her demeanor changed a moment later when he asked if he could throw her jeans over the chair to dry; she shot up so fast that she dropped the water bottle and immediately turned to steady herself against the foot of the bed nearby. There wasn't much room to maneuver in the tiny efficiency, but Gabe stepped back to show that he wasn't going to try anything.

"I'm sorry," he offered with his hands up like someone who was caught in the act of stealing. "I wasn't going to take them off or anything."

"No, I'm sorry," she breathed, sitting on the edge of the bed. "I just panicked." She accepted the bottle of water, which hadn't spilled because she still hadn't removed the cap.

"Do you want some sweatpants?" he asked instead. "I'll leave so you can change. Just yell when you're done."

"No, thanks...actually, yes. I'm sorry. I'm a mess tonight." She lay back in the bed, feet on the floor and body against the comforter, her hair still wrapped in the towel he'd given her.

He went into the bathroom and fidgeted with his phone while he waited, caught between wanting to get back to sleep and wanting to stay up later to make sure she'd be okay. When she yelled that she was dressed, he returned to find her sitting up in bed, a pillow wedged behind her back. She'd removed the shirt that she'd been wearing when she arrived to reveal a spaghetti-strap tank top. She looked more comfortable but still miserable, and he handed her a well-worn flannel to keep her warm.

"Thanks again," she mumbled, draping it over her shoulders.

"Of course. So, were you out with your roommates?" He didn't want to push, but he worried that this was a usual thing for Rebecca, and not just an isolated occurrence.

"Yeah," she said, the word turning into a yawn. She motioned him over and he lay next to her on his side, propping up his head with one arm so he could see her better. "I don't usually go this hard, but this week just..." She gestured vaguely. "I had another argument with my parents. Well, with my dad. Remember when I said my parents don't agree with how I live my life? It was...related to that."

Gabe reached out to hold her hand, and she let him. A long, comfortable silence ensued, and for a moment her eyes fluttered closed and he wondered if she'd fallen asleep. A moment later, though, she looked up again and reached for him with her free hand. She traced circles on his arm, and then higher, until her hand cupped the back of his head, and she leaned closer into him. He hesitated, conscious of her current state, and she pulled back to look him in the eye, a sudden, unexpected clarity emerging through the previous fog.

"It's okay," she whispered. "Really, I've wanted to. Please kiss me."

Despite his concern, he felt himself giving in. They kissed slowly, then again, and came apart for a breath only after sharing several more. She tasted like wine and licorice, and he realized that, at that moment, he wanted nothing more than to kiss her again.

So he did, and she let him. She moved closer, twining her legs around his, and as their kisses grew more impassioned, she breathed something against his lips, once, and then again: "*I want to tell you.*"

Reluctantly, but not without some excitement, Gabe slid back a bit so he could see her face. "You can tell me," he promised.

"I know, and I know you mean it, but I don't know how you'll react. It's pretty big news."

"You can tell me," he repeated firmly. "I promise you can."

She took his hand again and rubbed her thumb against his knuckles. "It's important for me to tell you, Gabe. And I have to before we go any further. Actually, I think I got drunk because I knew I wanted to tell you today. It wasn't just because I fought with my parents. We fight all the time anyway. But okay."

She continued slowly, in halting words. "I started going through some major changes when I was about twelve years old. I didn't know what was going on, but I knew something was, and I went to my mom, because I always went to her when I needed something. We were always close. But she reacted badly. Then she told my dad, and he was even worse. I lived with my grandparents for a full year because my dad couldn't look at me or talk to me.

"My grandparents took over for my parents. They made sure I was safe. They found doctors, and therapists, and they pleaded with my parents to be more supportive while I lived with them."

Gabe knew that if he interrupted, Rebecca might stop there. Instead, he waited, keeping quiet, until she picked up where she'd stopped.

"I like you, Gabe. And we've hung out a bit and had a great date, and I don't want to risk ruining this. Or changing your opinion of me. But if we're going to keep seeing each other, then you need to know that I'm trans."

Of everything that had blown through Gabe's mind during her sharing, this was something he'd never considered. It hadn't even occurred to him, even when she'd mentioned seeing doctors, that she might not be the cis woman his mind had filled her in as. The silence stretched on as his mind raced, and he tried to keep anything from being readable on his face as he thought.

"Gabe? Did you hear what I said?"

"Yes, sorry. I heard, I'm just... Wow. I'm just processing. I never would have guessed that. I mean..." But he didn't know how to complete the thought. This revelation should have changed everything he'd experienced with her, everything he'd felt—and she'd seemed to expect it to—but strangely, he found himself grappling only with the paradigm shift of his perception, not with the implications of the reality now that he knew.

Rebecca hadn't physically retreated during his silence, but she'd slid her hand out from his, and she seemed more alert now, as if in a fight-or-flight response. She flinched when he reached out to take her hand again, and her eyes widened when she realized he was going to kiss her again.

She held up a hand and gently stopped the kiss from happening. "Gabe, this is pretty big news. I don't want you to get swept up and then wake up tomorrow and decide it's too much."

"Has that happened before?" He didn't really want to know, but he knew that she deserved this time to explain, to confess, to protect herself.

"I *never* know how people are going to react. So, yeah, I've been ghosted, and insulted, and outed to people I didn't want to be out to. And sometimes guys get violent. Like they'll accuse me of trying to trap them or emasculate them or something. People get really insecure and lash out when they're caught by surprise, just because they think I'm pretty and then find out I have a..."

She gestured vaguely, and he tried to imagine how he'd be able to put himself out there, open himself up to someone he cared about, if the simple fact of his existence could put him in danger. He'd always considered himself to be a respectful, nonthreatening guy. When he walked home at night, he'd cross the street to give the entire sidewalk to a girl walking alone, just to reassure her that he wasn't a threat. He was tall, just over six feet, and still in decent shape from the sports he'd played in high school. He knew he could be imposing.

But for someone to have to worry about being attacked for their very identity, and one they hadn't even chosen but were forced to live with… It appalled him. He didn't want that constant uncertainty for her, and wouldn't want it for anyone, and he found himself wanting to share some of his own concerns in response.

"That's horrible," he said evenly. "For what it's worth, even though this isn't nearly the same thing, I was *this close* to changing high schools when I was a sophomore." He held his thumb and index finger barely apart to demonstrate. "I was…exploring things around that time, and I hooked up with this guy a couple of times. Then later, someone else I was interested in came onto me, and I was too naïve to think that it was a joke, or a trap. He found out that I was meeting up with a guy, and he invited me over to get me to admit it and out me, and life was horrible after that for a while."

"I'm so sorry, Gabe. Nobody should be forced to come out."

"That's true, and it scared me away from exploration for a long time. But my point is, I'm so glad you trusted me enough to tell me, and I'll have to adjust my thinking to think of you as the real you, now that I know, but I'm not afraid. I'm not one of the insecure guys who would be shocked or embarrassed to find out."

She moved her arm to rest behind his head again, and leaned forward until their foreheads were touching. "If you want to go on more dates, you understand that you'd be in a queer relationship, right? People would talk."

"I don't care about people talking."

"Your family would probably be surprised."

"They were also surprised when they walked in on me with a guy's hand down my pants when I was sixteen." He chuckled ruefully at the memory.

"You'd be immediately outed to anyone who knew I was trans—"

"Rebecca?"

"Sorry. Yes?"

"Please can I kiss you again?"

The following morning, a Wednesday, broke clear and bright, the rainclouds nowhere to be seen in the sky. Gabe woke when he felt Rebecca rise from the bed, and he watched through half-open eyes as she stood for a moment before the unfiltered sunlight coming in through the windows. He thought about everything that had transpired the previous night and smiled before giving in to the sleep he felt tugging at his consciousness again.

The gurgle of the coffeepot woke him a few minutes later, and he sat up with a groan but grinned when she turned to meet him with a coffee mug in her hands.

"Hi," she said simply, and took a careful sip from the mug.

"Good morning to you, too," he replied, sinking back into the sheets and checking the time on his phone. It was still early, barely nine o'clock, and he marveled at how rested he felt despite their late night together. "German starts in a bit. Are we going together, or do you need to get home first, or…?"

She shrugged. "Let's go together. My pants are mostly dried, but I'm stealing your socks and shirt. Don't argue," she added when he opened his mouth. "You were the hero last night, but I might still need one…or want one."

They walked into class holding hands, and when the lesson started, Gabe found it difficult to concentrate. He was too focused on the memory of how their fingers laced together; too distracted by everything he now knew about her, and the surprise he felt at how little it mattered in his perception of her. She was just *her*, and far from wanting to distance himself, he found himself eager to learn more about who she was.

He'd vaguely thought of himself as queer since his experiences in high school, but he'd never wondered about what that actually meant. He knew it meant—at least to him—that he could enjoy, or even love, someone other than a cis woman. In that sense, he'd always been open to a variety of partners, although, either by coincidence or some subconscious reluctance, most had been cis women.

But he didn't want to overanalyze this new attraction. He caught her glancing from the desk next to his and he covered his mouth to hide his grin. She did the same, and then jotted something on the side of her notebook closest to him. When the professor turned to the board, she slid the page closer to his desk: *I'm glad I can trust you.*

He wrote a note on his own page and angled it toward her: *Do you trust me enough to come over again soon?*

She added *Ja* beneath her first note.

"Sometimes I think we're all pretending out of necessity," Rebecca said a few days later. They were finishing lunch under the tallest, widest tree on North Campus, delighting in the cooling weather and the grass that had dried in the sun after the rain earlier in the week. She passed Gabe a piece of her blueberry muffin and he chewed it thoughtfully. He watched a bird fly by and rocket to a branch near the top of the tree.

"Pretending what?" he asked. "And for what reason?"

She picked at the rest of the muffin and watched the bird as it eyed their lunch. "I just think we *have* to pretend sometimes. Think of Sisyphus. He was made to push that boulder up a hill, only to have it roll back to the bottom every time he neared the top. It seems like a metaphor for…I don't know, being a functional adult. Everyone seems like they're constantly pushing their limits to improve their lives, and then once one goal is reached, they have a new one. We pretend it's normal, but why is there always a next step? Doesn't that stop us from being happy with what we have?"

"I feel like there's another metaphor in there somewhere," Gabe replied, choosing his words carefully. To his relief, she laughed.

"No, you're right. My life experience definitely colors how I view this stuff. It started with the easy aesthetic changes: my hair and clothes. Then I started hormones, and eventually I had minor FFS—sorry, facial feminization surgery. See, look"—she lifted her chin—"no Adam's apple. It was a lot of pain and discomfort, but seriously, I felt better about things afterward. Like I was finally seeing *me* in the mirror. But yeah. There's always something *else* out there, and there's *more* to yearn for that would help even more."

"You're beautiful." The words were out of his mouth barely after he'd thought them, but he didn't fumble or try to hide or add to them. It was the simple truth.

"You're sweet." She took his hand and kissed him, and again he marveled at this new physical closeness. She paused, about to say something else, and then closed her mouth.

"No, what?" he asked, not wanting to press but just wanting to hear her voice, to listen to her speak.

"That night at the Thai restaurant was my first real date as *me*. I had a great time, but I was worried that everyone was staring, even though I'm sure nobody was. You're a great date. I just wanted you to know that."

"Hey…so are you. It was nice."

With that, they lay together on the grass, still holding hands, and watched the sun filter through the changing leaves and the birds come and go.

All the leaves on the trees, Gabe thought distantly. *They look so pretty after they've changed.* Because *they've changed.* He thought there might be a poem in there somewhere, maybe related to autumn but maybe not. He was still thinking about it when Rebecca turned to look at him, her smile causing him to flush with delight and match it with his own.

That night, Gabe's phone buzzed sometime after nine while he trudged through *Gulliver's Travels* for homework. He'd already eaten dinner, and the sun had set hours before. He read the new text from Rebecca: *Can I come up? I'm not even drunk this time.*

Sure! On my way, he replied, and then: *Everything okay?*

Her response came immediately. *I just wanted to kiss you.*

Once upstairs, she set down her bag and did just that. There were few places to sit in the tiny apartment, other than the secondhand loveseat in front of the television, so he allowed her to lead him to the bed and gently pull him down. They lay side by side, each kiss faster and more passionate than the last, and paused only long enough to pull their shirts off.

He'd never seen so much of her skin before, and he committed each detail to memory as he ran his fingers down her back: her lithe, toned torso; the portrait of a veiled woman tattooed on her shoulder; the bare tree with falling leaves suspended in midair on her right upper arm.

Then she turned and pulled him on top of her, and he didn't think of anything at all.

"I like the naked tree on your arm," Gabe told Rebecca later, as they cuddled in bed and watched an old sitcom on Netflix.

"Thanks! It's actually the one that has the most meaning to me. When I lived with my grandparents, they would play an old Nick Drake record called *Five Leaves Left*. There are a few songs on that album that really kept me sane during that year, so look." She turned her arm so he could see the details better. "Five leaves."

He kissed them and followed her arm up to kiss her shoulder and neck. "I'm glad you had someone to help you through everything."

"Me too, believe me. But you know what I need to get me through now?"

"What's that?"

"Something to eat. But I'm not leaving this bed anytime soon, so who delivers here?"

Gabe laughed aloud at that and slid out of bed to find his phone. He read off the options, and while she considered, he leaned against the wall and watched the traffic light outside the building flash red at the intersection. This late, it stopped cycling through its colors and just acted as a stop sign, and in the intermittent red light, he turned from the window to the woman in his bed. As she scrolled through the Netflix menu, he imagined where their relationship might take them, and he smiled inwardly.

It could lead them anywhere, he knew, but for the moment, he was just glad it had brought them here.

From the Author

The motivation for "All the Leaves in the Trees" originally came from a desire to write about a couple of separate experiences that were meaningful to me in different ways. The story itself isn't a "true" account of anything that happened in exactly the same way, but the fundamental events, more or less, do come from my memory. The resulting amalgamation holds a unique significance to me, both because writing it allowed me to honor several people I used to know, and because the inspiration for the story shaped me in different ways.

I say "people I used to know" because none of the inspirations for the character of Rebecca remain in my present-day life. Sadly, one passed away several years ago. Another I lost contact with even longer ago.

I hope the timidity and boldness of Rebecca's character resonates with some readers. At her core, I think she is vulnerable because she wants to know that it's safe to be, and bold because she's learned to put up a defensive exterior to protect her identity.

Likewise, I hope Gabriel's cluelessness and openness offer some kind of hope for readers who feel, or have felt, discouraged or alone or simply not accepted. Neither character is perfect, and both have their insecurities and problems to navigate. However, the relationship they form by the end of the story is one of trust, respect, and acceptance. Sometimes, that alone is more than we can dare to hope for, but the story is meant to extend some kind of hope that we can find it in the future.

—David J. Vane, April 2024

About the Author

David J. Vane teaches college English in the northeastern United States, where he lives with his partner, son, and two cats. He is a consistent advocate for LGBTQ rights and equity. In his free time, David enjoys playing the guitar and watching or reading horror. He can be reached at Davidjvane19@gmail.com and welcomes feedback and questions about his work.

From the Editors

From Sam Knight

In March of 2023, my friend L.J. Hachmeister published a successful charity anthology, *Instinct: An Animal Rescuers Anthology*, to raise money for a no-kill puppy shelter. It was set up so that a minimum of 50% of all royalties would go to the puppy rescue with even more donated if the contributors chose to donate more. Which some did. (Somewhere around 70% goes to the shelter. I don't have access to the accounts where I would see the exact numbers.)

When the anthology finally released, L.J. had posted in a private group, "My dream is to sell 10,000 in the first week—which would put us at saving about 1,000 puppies."

She accomplished that in 2 days. (Which, if the anthology would have been "traditionally" published, would have put it on pretty much any bestseller list.)

L.J. passed away less than a month later. She did not get to see that the first check Lifeline Puppy rescue received was for almost $37,000. She did not get to learn that in the year since then, they have received almost that much again.

To the best of my knowledge, L.J. received little to no compensation for the work she put into the anthology, and, unfortunately, her medical bills were not small. My hope for this anthology is that it raises some money to help L.J.'s widow with some of those bills. The truth is, I know most anthologies earn very little money. But, at the very least, I hope it buys her a cup of coffee and lets her know someone else cared too.

I am very proud of L.J.'s accomplishment and honored that she asked me to contribute and be a part of it.

Once upon a time, years before L.J. asked me to help her edit and publish that anthology, she had asked me to write her a story about two lesbians meeting for the first time and falling in love. I laughed, and she said she was serious. She really wanted to see what I would write.

I started one, but lost the file somewhere, somehow, as sometimes happens to even those of us who back them up fastidiously, and then never went back to rewrite and finish it. Which means L.J. never got to read it. That's an ache in my heart that will never heal.

In another random conversation with L.J., the kind authors have with each other where we ramble from Star Wars to Marvel to Poe and then the Bible and then Snickerdoodle Cookies, she told me that when she was growing up there weren't enough of those kinds of stories (lesbians meeting and falling in love), and she felt that if she would have had them as guidelines/role models, it would have helped her a lot. (In yet a different personal conversation, she talked about the intense stress of asking another girl out, not knowing how the girl would react.)

Talking to other authors who knew her, it turns out I wasn't the only one she'd asked to write that kind of a story for her.

She was looking for them. Even years later, she was, I think, still seeking validation in the reflection of herself, of people like her, in fictional stories.

Which is what so many of us read fiction for. Yes, it's a great way to have adventures or go to far off planets or meet mermaids and ride unicorns, but... But it is a way for us to learn, grow, and explore our own thoughts, feelings, ideas, values, and, maybe most importantly, self-identity.

There are tons of boy meets girl stories that we see and hear, all the time, from the moment we can start paying attention. From famous novels and movies to TV shows and commercials. And for the people those stories are applicable to, they are "lessons" or templates for those kinds of interactions, for how the boy and girl can, or should, or could, interact, even when fictitious and obviously untrue.

But for the rest of us who do not fall easily into the boy/girl combination, there are very few examples of "How do I meet them?" "What do I say?" "How can I tell if they like me, or even if they are like me?" "How do I deal with...?"

And those are tough questions for anyone, let alone people who don't have good examples to learn from, who don't have easy guidelines to follow, who don't have any experience to build upon.

And, over time, and to my naive, mostly tone-deaf ears, L.J. had indirectly (or I guess very directly) told me that she had needed that. That she had still needed it.

So, in her memory, in her honor, and to help support her widow and maybe cover some of L.J.'s medical bills, I began to put together an anthology of the kinds of positive role-model stories I thought she was looking for. Though, as L.J. was one of the most accepting people I have ever known (though she didn't suffer mean people very well!), I wasn't restricting it to lesbian stories. I was looking for first time meetings of people who fall anywhere on the all-inclusive LBGTQ+ spectrum, that lead to healthy relationships. I wanted stories about her. About people like her. About people like her in the fact that they felt different like she felt different. I wanted stories that could possibly help people who might need a guiding example or reassurance that they aren't alone.

So, for the anthology, I asked for romantic stories of meeting and falling in love, though I recognized that did not fully apply to everyone or may not apply in the same way to everyone.

And that was the heart of the issue for L.J., I think, in asking for a story from her author friends. Not everything does apply to everyone. And for those trying to find their way, a good story about a particular path that actually does apply to them may mean everything to them.

And I hoped I could help provide some of that. If not for L.J., then for someone else who needed it.

It turned out to be a lot more difficult than I thought. Part of it, I am sure, was that I was asking people to donate half (or more) of their earnings for the stories. But then I ran into a different, unexpected issue. So many, many of the submissions we received were completely off target. Stories that were definitely not positive role models. Stories that were not LGBTQIA+. Stories that were not even about relationships. In and of itself, that is not too unusual. Open submissions (aka "slush piles") are notoriously full of... How to put this kindly? Stuff no one wants to read and often regrets having done so afterward.

The really difficult part was that we received an unusually low number of submissions that were on theme. So much so, we had to re-open submissions with a wider theme of LGBTQIA+ stories, looking more for representation.

Because that's what we are really talking about here. Representation. And I hope we have managed to add to the many steps being taken by so many people in an attempt to normalize that, to create stories that show a reader that they are "not alone" in who they are, and to help those kinds of stories become commonplace.

A few people have told me that the kinds of stories I was originally looking for do exist now, and that they are easy to find. Any young person needing "representation" can find a story about someone like themselves easily nowadays, unlike when L.J. was young and couldn't.

My personal experience would seem to contradict that. I think that it may seem true at first blush, but I think most of the stories out there are probably not representative of a positive role model. I hope I am wrong.

Meanwhile, I also hope something, somewhere in this anthology helps someone. Even if it is only to take their mind off problems for a few minutes while they escape into a story.

I would like to take a moment and thank the people who donated their work to make this happen.

First, I would sincerely like to thank my Co-Editor, Katie Kent. There are so many reasons why this anthology would never have been possible without her. I can't thank you enough, Katie.

I would like to thank Kim May, Lucas Stagg, and Cherrie Lynn Fors for reading along with us. Pat Smythe for cleaning up the spilled word salad. And Nicci Peschel for the wonderful cover.

And, of course, I want to thank the authors, for putting up with the time it took to make this happen. For sending us stories. And for donating half (or more) of their royalties.

If you enjoyed their stories, please reach out to them. Let them know. Interact on social media with them. Honestly, writing can be like sitting alone in a dark hole, and having someone reach out to say they liked what you did can be like the sudden appearance of the sun and a golden staircase leading to an exquisite banquet in a hall full of dancing aristocrats who stop and applaud because they all love you.

Am I exaggerating? Kind of, but not really. I have watched authors cry as they recounted stories of a reader telling them how their stories impacted them and their lives. Just as I have seen readers cry when trying to tell an author how much something meant to them. Sometimes, an author gets it right. Sometimes they manage to represent you. Or what you want to be. Or what you're going through.

Stories are magic. If someone tells you one that is magic for you, you need to let them know. That may be the encouragement they need to write the next story that will be magic for someone else.

Thank you for purchasing this anthology. It means a lot to me.

Sam Knight
April, 2024

From Katie Kent

It was some time last year when I reached out to Sam to ask him for some advice regarding a novel I was writing. Sam had published a few of my stories in his anthologies, and the reason I asked him, rather than any other publishers I had worked with, was the positive impression he'd made on me. Not all publishers send carefully considered edits to stories. Some of them publish the stories exactly as they are when accepted, typos and all. Sam's approach marked him out to me as someone knowledgeable, someone easy to talk to, and someone who cared about the quality of the anthologies he produces.

After giving me his thoughts on the question I'd asked him, he noted that me getting in contact with him was spooky timing, as he had been meaning to contact me to ask me about an anthology he was thinking about putting together in honour of a writer friend who had recently passed away—L.J. Hachmeister. Whilst being an experienced small publisher, Sam did not have experience with the topic of the anthology, whereas he knew that the majority of stories I write are LGBTQIA+ romance stories. I was honoured to be asked to help Sam edit this anthology, and want to thank him for all the support and guidance he gave me throughout the process. I am sad I never got to know L.J., but am pleased that I got to work on a project for such a good cause. I hope it gives her widow at least some small comfort.

I was 22 when I came out. I suffered from social anxiety and low self-esteem as a child, and kept my same sex attractions to myself. I look on my university years as a lost opportunity to be myself—instead, I spent two of the three years pining over another girl on my course, whilst giving no one any indication that I was anything other than straight. As well as my social anxiety, I was at university in the late 90s, when it still seemed slightly taboo to be different in that way. I was always a voracious reader, and would have loved to have read an anthology like this. Maybe it would have helped me see that there was nothing wrong with me, that different didn't mean bad. At the very least I know I would have appreciated reading stories about people like me. These days, more people realise how important it is to recognize people like yourself in the stories you read. One of the reasons I tend toward writing young adult stories is probably because part of me has never grown up; part of me is still that young adult who struggled with her sexuality, the teenager who never felt completely at home in her own body.

In this anthology we have stories from ten talented writers, in addition to the stories from me and Sam. I enjoyed reading every single story, getting to know the characters as they took their first steps toward romance. We have a real mix of genres, from contemporary to science fiction, fantasy and horror. Thank you for buying the anthology, and I hope you enjoy reading it as much as I've enjoyed working on it.

Katie Kent
April 2024

Additional Copyright Information

www.ingramcontent.com/pod-product-compliance
Lightning Source LLC
Chambersburg PA
CBHW031059020726
47495CB00007B/1954